ARCADE PUBLISHING
NEW YORK

THE AGONIES

A NOVEL

BEN FAULKNER

Copyright © 2025 by Ben Faulkner

All rights reserved. No part of this book may be reproduced in any manner without the express written consent of the publisher, except in the case of brief excerpts in critical reviews or articles. All inquiries should be addressed to Arcade Publishing, 307 West 36th Street, 11th Floor, New York, NY 10018.

Arcade Publishing books may be purchased in bulk at special discounts for sales promotion, corporate gifts, fund-raising, or educational purposes. Special editions can also be created to specifications. For details, contact the Special Sales Department, Arcade Publishing, 307 West 36th Street, 11th Floor, New York, NY 10018 or arcade@skyhorsepublishing.com.

Arcade Publishing® is a registered trademark of Skyhorse Publishing, Inc.®, a Delaware corporation.

Visit our website at www.arcadepub.com.

Please follow our publisher Tony Lyons on Instagram @tonylyonsisuncertain

10 9 8 7 6 5 4 3 2 1

Library of Congress Cataloging-in-Publication Data is available on file.

Cover design by David Ter-Avanesyan
Cover Image from *The Last Judgement* by Michelangelo

Print ISBN: 978-1-64821-118-8
Ebook ISBN: 978-1-64821-119-5

Printed in the United States of America

Vouchsafe unto me a mask of anger.
—Osamu Dazai, *No Longer Human*

THE END OF MY FAMILY

My mother died in June.
In the basement I watched a blurry horror movie from 1974. A man in overalls tied a lost teenager to train tracks. The boy's death was symbolized by churning sounds and a horn as the killer watched from a nearby car. My dad crashed in like a mass shooting survivor. "No, he doesn't have a phone. Right. No, he doesn't even own a phone." His shining eyes were from a greeting card sketch of a depressed dog, something in a faded memory. "Your aunt needs to talk to you." I hate talking on phones, but the way he said it . . .

"Hello," I said.

My mom was dead? Huh?

I handed back the phone without finishing the conversation and ran upstairs, three at a time like retard slenderman.

My bedroom was a deserted hellhole. An open window stirred trash around. My dad called my shitty name up the steps, and I sat there, blank, like paranormal activity in the black mirror of my TV. At a "Now Loading" screen, thoughts floated up, activating dead parts of my brain like a flashlight in an abandoned house. My character—"Cloud Strife"—wandered around a lonely city, and the feelings died.

It's good to have feelings, but first responses are pure static. Like how the present moment is just a whirr of emotion, burying the wrongness of everyone's choices, proven by the way hairstyles and pop songs are later revealed to be failures of good taste. "It's probably not even true," I said, tensing every muscle and clenching my teeth until I vibrated. The controller squeaked in my hand like a video of someone crushing hamsters. My mom is dead? Judy, my aunt, didn't seem to know what happened. She said something about—forget it. I let go. From that day's viewpoint, my mother's death was just another unproven theory like "controlled demolition."

Final Fantasy VII is a Japanese role-playing game from 1997. There was a modern remake a couple years ago, but I had been playing the original on a tiny CRT monitor designed for use in medical procedures. I spray-painted the TV red but that seemed try-hard, and I regretted it. Everything in my room has to be old. At least fifteen years old but twenty to twenty-five years seems better, purer; too old (thirty-plus years) seems distracting, corny, try-hard. The presence of old objects is a drug that helps. If you put enough old things together it works like a magic circle and you can exit the present year, until someone invades the ambiance, shattering the illusion. It was working, barely. I was in a dream—

My dad barged in again.

"Are you ready to go?" he said. He was dressed like a midlife crisis in skinny jeans and a scarf.

"Am I ready for what?"

"Are you ready to go?"

"Go where?"

"I think we should be with your mother's family."

"I don't want to go anywhere," I said. "I don't want to be around people."

"You don't have to."

He walked down the steps and I heard the door.

I was thinking about yelling, I know I don't have to go anywhere, I'm an adult, why would I be forced to go places, but that would just be rude, plus he seemed like he was about to have a heart attack. At least he didn't block the TV. Not because the TV is more important (it's not), but because it's obnoxious to assume I want to deal with this rather than distracting myself to make everything easier for everyone. Outside the too-bright window, he was kneeling on the lawn like a crazy person praying to the road. Why does he care? They divorced. More to the point, why is life such an embarrassing disaster? I kicked the TV off the table and it crashed onto the floor. My existence was thirty-three percent avoidance, thirty-three percent pointless affect, and thirty-three percent massive errors, but everything else, literally everything else in the entire world, was somehow even worse.

Now this.

DEAD MOTHER

My mom's death was on the front page of *The New York Times*. They described her as an essayist and memoirist, noted for her "celebrated examinations of women's lives." My dad had been published as much as my mom, but if he died, they probably wouldn't put him in *The New York Times*. Mostly because he's a white-presenting cis male. I'm not saying that in a complaining or aggrieved way, just that I don't believe they would. It's not a big deal to me, but it's just, honoring female writers is perceived to be a more fashionable and worthwhile gesture than honoring white male writers to the middlebrow, normie, fake-cultured people who work for *The New York Times*. I don't have an opinion on whether that's good or bad; it's merely a feature of current-day life in America so obvious and boring it's hard to form a strong feeling about. Also, I could be wrong. They might feature him. Who cares? Maybe if he died they would be obsessed with him. I've stopped trying to predict everything and if I'm wrong about every thought I've ever had, I'm extremely sorry. Genuinely.

My mother's obituary seemed designed to stir melancholy feelings in the reader. She had been "survived" by her son it said near the end. The piece read as cloying, to me. For people more famous than my mother they have something ready to print at the moment of death, but no one bothered to anticipate this (how could they) and it arrived several days late. If she died gradually instead of being murdered they might have planned it better. The first time I read it, it seemed impossible to understand, like a jumble of words that symbolized nothing. Then I tried again and it made me cry, mostly because I was drifting, minute by minute, away from a world I had a mother in.

Plus the word "murder" jabbed at something, making my family sound like more of a disturbing car crash than before.

I have a fear of becoming more alien, more adrift, and I sometimes make myself cry to feel I'm caught up behaviorally, like a man who sends taxes in late, hoping the IRS won't bash his skull in.

But my feelings that week were real—in fact, what really bothered me was that she used to have a voice, a literal voice that made specific sounds, a completely unique and unrepeatable natural phenomenon, and it was gone, just removed, like a secret someone destroyed all evidence of. That concept was canyon-like, and 4 AM-like, and solitary, and bottom of the ocean-like, and outer space–like, and empty movie theatre–like, and dungeon-like, and attic-like, and dead animal–like, and raindrop-like, and blue. It gave me the feeling of a pet running away or a tiny heart-shaped balloon disappearing in a cloud. Sorry to be pretentious, but do you know what I mean? Does anyone?

I didn't go to her funeral because I didn't have the right kind of clothes, plus I didn't want anyone to ask me about what college I was going to (I wasn't going) or call me the YouTube star. Plus, everyone expected me to go, and that sort of thing makes me completely unwilling to participate. There was no reason I needed to be there, and in some ways ignoring it seemed normal too, like he's really suffering and it's all too much to take. I told myself they wouldn't judge me though they probably did. If I didn't have to see them, it didn't matter. The worst of all was YouTube star, I felt like if people called me a YouTube star I was going to die. The videos weren't even up anymore. I don't know why anyone cared anyway. It was so stupid. I also didn't want anyone to say my name. I hated my name but hadn't thought of a replacement yet.

I cried for the third time during her funeral. My too-silent room stirred irrational emotion. Why was I even sad? She got everything she wanted from a fake and pointless life. She was even in *The New York Times*. I shouldn't criticize. Everything in life is irrational. I'm no better; I just filter life through a shellac of ironic hate and self-conscious, stylized contempt. Instead of going to college, I was going to work on that. I finally had a goal. Then I might actually know what's worthwhile and could climb ahead of almost everyone, but in a logical way worth caring about. My dad told me we would be going on vacation soon for two weeks. I don't normally agree to do things like that, but I have been depressed and need to hit reset or something, and fast. Otherwise, I'll be dead at nineteen and it won't even be a tragedy.

On the day of the funeral, my dad came home late. He knocked and said, "How are you?" I didn't respond and the light under the door went dark. In bed, I thought: If my life adds up to ninety-nine percent (avoidance, affect, and errors) what is the remaining one percent? Maybe a secret, even to me—a darkly incubating, seedlike future I'll eventually become. In reality my life didn't add up to ninety-nine percent, or anything at all. A ghost of headlights slid across the ceiling and I could hear the stars outside. They sounded like sex toys disgusting middle-aged women use, or, in a more tolerable image, a Nintendo 64 Rumble Pak? In any case they were buzzing, murmuring. They said, Words are words—numbers and letters are words too. Huh? I was picking up on something and putting it together. Life is a viewfinder, a B movie attached to a primitive force feedback device with no meaning attached. Or maybe that's only true of average people. I will develop myself and become glass, and then air. I will become perfect and patent a way to really be free.

Someone else will die.

My life, a dreamlife, will never end.

JOTTINGS

What is a family?
Do you have love for me?
I'm just kidding.

Four years ago, a sixteen-year-old shot up the private high school I barely graduated from a few months ago. Other than the shooter, only one kid was killed. It only briefly caught the attention of national news. The most interesting aspect was the choice to scratch his suicide note onto a blackboard. I was in gym class when everyone poured out screaming. Then the police rushed in and killed him. It was a big scene at 10 AM, but when I wandered back in the middle of the night under a phlegmy full moon that made the whole world look like a parking lot, there was no trace. No clue–like objects to take home and keep. I'm not sure what I was expecting, but the ordinariness of the scene disturbed me, the way terrible events are absorbed in a spongelike way rather than leaving a stain. About the blackboard, the killer was blurred in the bodycam video due to being a minor—giving the video a literally ghostly quality—but if you paused it at exactly the right second you could read the stuff he wrote in white chalk:

What is a family?
Do you have love for me?
I'm just kidding.

There were other elliptical questions and comments, like a psychotic parody of an old-fashioned blackboard punishment. Below his final earthly statement, he drew a frowny face with a tear below its eye and a halo over its head.

We were off school for ten days after the shooting. My dad seemed pleased about the whole thing because, he said, it proved rich white county kids are as dangerous as black city kids, a slightly "libtard" idea he used to be fixated on. I wanted to say that if you really believed that you wouldn't have sent me there, but instead said the kid was half-Hispanic, like you. My dad responded by saying it was a white crime even if it was committed by a non-white kid. Why is that? I asked. Because it was done indiscriminately, and with a rifle, in a symbolically evil rather than reckless spirit. His statement had a politically incorrect feeling, even though it was designed to seem politically correct. Still, I agreed. It was a white crime. White people commit mass shootings in a dazed and brokenhearted mood, indicating an inability to cope—think some burst of chaotic violence, then suicide by cop. White mass murder is a deformed artistic gesture. Black gun violence is a paean to personal strength in the face of insurmountable odds and the numbing logic of the modern world, whereas white violent crime is an investigation of disturbing textures and emotion? One is about the failure of an individual to develop in a creative mode; the other is a failure to develop in professional culture. Both acts share a vaguely common sense of frustration, but white mass murder is more dangerous because it more directly condemns society, like an underground work of self-taught philosophy. Black murder is more like a depressing department store going out of business ("liquidation sale"), or maybe sports, or pornography. Hispanic murder was, well, I wasn't sure yet, but probably something else altogether, perhaps a haunted carnival or apocalyptic drug party in the desert. I began to explain these ideas, but my dad's expression told me I had unwittingly taken another wrong turn. For the five-thousandth time I apologized for another unacceptable thought, then went to bed.

A few months ago, I had this invasive thought that the words on the blackboard were actually something the teacher wrote, some part of a lesson the shooter interrupted. This never occurred to me because I had initially read the language as eerie and elliptical. But interpreting such bland, Rorschach test–like writing as creepy was merely a quirk of framing and context. I used to work on writing but gave it up when I realized how similar my efforts were to that kid's final scribbled statements on the blackboard.

> *I'm sorry.*
> *Am I screwy?*
> *I'm fucked up.*
> *Am I stupid?*

Again, it wasn't homage, I thought, but maybe in some unconscious sense, it was, like how painters and musicians copy their peers without even noticing. I tried to look up the bodycam video again, but it had been removed from

YouTube. The internet is apparently forever, but this video was really gone. I tried to read about the crime instead but couldn't find much. The information seemed to be fading, the way a newspaper would get if it sat in the sun for several months. Soon, everyone involved with the crime will be forgotten, and the crime will have no moral feeling at all, like the tale of some long-ago hurricane or snowstorm. I was left wondering this: what is the difference between the scrawled message turning out to be a suicide note or classroom lesson? That depends on your idea of reality. If we really do occupy a communal and shared concrete reality, then it means a lot. One is canonical and true, and the other is not. On the other hand, if reality only exists privately, like a dream, or the picture in a VR headset, then it means nothing. Most people discount that latter idea—that life is a hallucination, or like a hallucination, unique to each individual and carved from ghostly materials—but when I had my psychotic break twenty some months ago, it became clear how distinctly possible that strange concept actually is. I sometimes want to reinvestigate the theory, prod at it more systematically, but it represents a very destabilizing mental alley I don't feel safe exploring.

I flipped through my old notebook—pages and pages of inane remarks that once seemed profound:

Are you really there?
You are sorry for having me.
How long will I be alive for?

I wrote a bunch more crap before giving up. When that section ended there was a short story written from the perspective of a homunculus called "My Life in Acid Rain (Homunculus)." It had more literary potential than everything else but similarly went nowhere. On the notebook's final page there was an oily stain where I crushed a fake homunculus on camera. My video was called *I Made a Homunculus*. It was a parody of another popular video from that era where a man in a gas mask created a seemingly real homunculus. First he injected an egg with his semen, then days later extracted a sluglike blob with tweezers. Finally he crushed it under a Russian language textbook. I did something similar but in a zanier, parodic tone. I don't remember how many views my hilarious parody video got before being deleted, but I remember some of the comments telling me how funny they found it. It didn't include the short story written from the creature's perspective, which began with:

> *My Life in Acid Rain (Homunculus)*
> *I was born in January, and I die in January.*
> *My life in acid rain.*
> *My life in acid rain.*
> *My life in acid rain.*

It went on and on like that before transitioning into a rambling paragraph about personal desire and the meaning of life.

Great stuff, huh? What the fuck was I thinking?

I threw the notebook in the trash. I didn't want to see it again. It literally hurt my head and made my vision seem bleached—literally fade—to see creative efforts I once attempted. I was hoping to straighten up my room, but I was too mentally fucked to keep working.

We're going on vacation tomorrow.

I'll feel better when we get back.

RIDE

It's been almost two months since my mom died. I care less and less. It wasn't such a big deal. It was the symbology most of all. "Your mother was murdered." What a statement, like the plot of a movie more so than my life, worse even than the thing itself. Is a statement differentiated from the fact it represents, or are they one unsettling statistic? Ultimately, I wasn't sure I even understood the question and let it go. Being in the woods, maybe I would hear from her ghost. I didn't exactly believe in that, but I didn't exactly not. In this world almost anything is possible. The question is whether one can apprehend the amorphous and superreal side of life without completely dissolving in false positives. As for me, I failed at that task and became lost. The memory of two years ago—my eleventh grade breakdown—was too much like staring at an eclipse and I let that thought go too.

I squinted at the green brushstroke of undifferentiated foliage (I like the druggy blur of highway scenery) in an attempt to see everything vaguely, like through textured glass, as I consciously thought about nothing.

"What do you think your moral belief system is?" my dad asked me, messing up my concentration.

He was listening to slightly corny, slightly soothing Gen X music, like "Wilco" but not. The singer was going on and on in a try-hard, fake-emotional way.

"What?" I said.

"What do you think your moral belief system is?" my dad asked me.

"I don't know," I said.

"One time you said you thought people have a moral obligation to commit suicide."

"I did?"

It was quiet in the car. "Do you like this music?" He turned it up.

"No," I said. "I hate this music."

"Why?"

"Because it is a rip-off of other things, and I don't even like the things it is ripping off."

"What is it ripping off?"

"Everything else you listen to."

I imagined a bunch of bloated middle-aged white men who dressed like my dad pretending to be rock stars and "hitting the road for Biden," or something similarly blandly political and absurd. I caught myself falling into a preordained role just as they had: the surly, mentally ill teen who is unnecessarily rude. "This music is good," I said. "This music is fine. All music is equally good. I like all music equally." I could read his mind. My dad was thinking, "Armie is in a bad mood." But I wasn't. I was literally just trying to have a conversation and communicate accurately. The problem maybe was that I did genuinely view him with contempt. I barely even viewed him as human.

In some essential way I had already lost both of them.

VACATION

Someone said, I am a warrior, so that my son may be a merchant, so that his son may be a poet. In my family, the cycle has been completed. What comes next? A cliff's edge, or the return of the warrior?

Our two-week vacation was calm. Moody and atmospheric, as well. More consequentially, it resulted in progress. In this way it was a perfect experience. Enjoyable, but also containing an event that advances my life. Life is, it seems, rather than constant forward progress, periods of stasis, then some changing event, introducing a new moment or phase. The trigger can be good or bad, pleasurable or traumatic, catastrophe or lucky chance. Or, like in my case, pure epiphany. Even quiet epiphany, less a bright light than a dimly illuminated blur, like a firefly crushed against a wall in a dark backyard.

My event was simply this thought: I'm not getting anything out of life and so, I should try. If I try, my feeling of getting nothing out of life may end. If I don't try, no such possibility can ever arise. There was a flaw in the argument (why care about "getting something out of life") but the drive contained some feeling of truth for me, and I made vague plans to enact it.

The setting was a cabin by a lake. The lush summer woods had a vintage slasher movie quality. *The Burning. Sleepaway Camp. Friday the 13th.* I walked around and found deserted shacks. In a spergy way, I imagined I was some killer, my life, a POV sequence, but there was no straight razor or teenagers to kill, just jumbles of plants and empty rooms. I found little objects in the dirt and watched my hand reach out to grab them. I crucially lacked a black leather glove. When I got sweaty, I wandered back and turned on the air-conditioning. My dad mostly sat outside; he took notes and read books. There was no TV or cell phone reception, which didn't bother me. I don't use that stuff anyway. I try to live in the past, and there is no one in the world I want to be contacted by.

We drove to a beach two hours away. There was a seagull with a broken wing in the parking lot. I wanted to find a wildlife rehabilitator and have it fixed. I felt surprised by the clarity and force of my drive to do "the right thing" in this situation. The bird waddled under a car. When I kneeled and looked, it was gone, like a magic trick. My dad called for me, I said, it's over here. He walked over, but the bird really was gone. It had outsmarted me, or actually outsmarted itself, because I only wanted to help. The animal was wise to view people warily. It had no reason to think I wouldn't break its other wing and leave it in a heap for laughs. Why was I not such a person? Why was my morality calibrated exactly at the point where I would help a bird but slash a person's throat? Would I actually? I fantasized about doing exactly that as I wandered through the woods. Was that real, or merely a way of seeing myself as hard, when in truth I am soft? One day I would do some terrifying act, as a proof, if it made sense, if I could get away with it, if the person had earned it . . .

The bird really was injured. Where did it go? It bothers me still. I should have spent more time. I should have tried. That animals are made to pointlessly suffer is reason enough to hate the world. By not trying I was as disgraceful as everyone else. I lack the potential to help an animal or harm a man. If I can't change that, I am less than nothing and owe it to virtue itself to end my life.

In the evenings my father and I drove to the little town—really just a solitary street with a few boring shops and diners—to get food then go back. My dad made fires. We sat there mutely.

"What are you working on?" I asked him.

"A book."

"What's it about?"

"Family."

That sounded stupid but I didn't say anything. My dad's first book was about being the son of a Colombian immigrant. It was really dumb.

The next day my dad's girlfriend drove to the cabin. She ate lunch with us. She and my dad left. "I'll be back tomorrow. You don't mind, right?"

My dad is a good-looking, slightly swarthy writer. He looks like the Canadian Prime Minister, Justin Trudeau. Someone stupid literally thought he was Justin Trudeau at a restaurant in Baltimore. "Are you Justin Trudeau?" the woman asked. I laughed and he became embarrassed. Later, he called me "rude." He does things like make fires, play guitar, talk about leftist politics, quote Plato. It is a corny persona white women like. Men's wives eye him up and down when we're out. My parents split up due to fighting too much, but there was more to it, something the fights revealed that was absolutely repulsive. She was dead now. Maybe in the future I would confront what I found out about them. It was another aspect of life I hated to look directly at.

Just before noon. 85 degrees. I wandered away. The damp forest. I sat against a tree. I brought a book. *L'Étranger*. In tenth grade I taught myself French. My school didn't offer it, so I taught myself. Not that well. I could barely read a book Camus deliberately composed in a plain and simple voice. My dad even paid for lessons. The tutor was shocked I was learning French on my own. I think he thought I was insane or a genius. I was neither. I merely had an interest in Rimbaud and existentialism at that time, not really knowing anything about them, just randomly identifying with some books I found in the basement.

    I held the book into a crease of light, like a ritual bowl for catching blood, and tried to read, but couldn't really. It was so pretentious and affected to read this in French. I buried the book under some soil and leaves so it might rot in an accelerated way. I was beginning to think about writing. My writing was terrible. Maybe if I actually tried . . .

    I walked to the edge of the woods. There was a campsite, an Airstream camper, and some people my age. The vehicle glinted in the overwhelming light like a killer's knife. The people chased each other around, laughing. They seemed genuinely joyous. At what? Just being young and social and happy. They weren't worried about identifying some logical basis with which to justify their joy. Whether or not they were allowed to feel happy based on some strange criteria they held all experience up to. It simply was. They simply did.

I tell myself that gatherings and celebrations are false, people putting on airs, enacting incredible labors to implant, in a fundamentally false way some image in a stranger's mind about what they are, what they want to be seen as. These people were not that. They were undeniably the thing they were presenting as. The image perfectly lined up with the reality of their experience—joy, real joy at being here with one another. I felt ashamed to watch them like this. Often, I felt above average people. Today, I felt very much below. I had been happy at one time. Until eleventh grade. Until being cursed. I hadn't really been cursed. Right? For a time I believed I had been. I just needed to try.

As we drove back home, I said, "I'm going to get a job."

"You don't have to do that yet," he said. "You could restart your YouTube channel or take just a couple classes somewhere or something."

My YouTube channel? Why would someone think it's a better idea to be an exhibitionist on camera, generating revenue for Google, instead of something old-fashioned and normal and healthy-seeming, like a job?

"I think it would be good for me," I said.

"Well, if that's what you want to do, I'll be proud of you," he said. "Where do you want to work?"

"I don't know yet."

WORK

Where would I work? We live in an upper-middle-class suburb in Baltimore. The obvious thing would be to walk to the vaguely "cool" but essentially middlebrow neighborhood and work as a dishwasher or clerk in a "tasteful" alternative-culture coded business. That neighborhood is right down the street, and I seem like one of those people. Someone trying to be assimilated, observing social cues and temporal cultural phases and styles, reflecting, refracting them back, slightly processed through my "individuality," but intact and recognizable. Why do I seem like that? I don't know, I just do. Partly my clothes. I wear bummy clothes with holes and paint spatter. I prefer thick and baggy clothing, faded stuff. Everything should be at least twenty years old. Just plain cotton items. Or military-issue or camouflage. But not obnoxious. Calibrating the effect toward quiet and vague, ostensibly indifferent. I would like to tone that down, dress in a way that exudes, somehow, nothing. I have a look that seems too participatory, but I don't really have the will to change it.

Despite seeming like one, I dislike artist types. They project pride in a way that repulses me. Dressing up their stupid indulgences for public consumption. Only partly self-aware as they drag the most lamentable tendencies of adolescents—clubby in-group fixation, self-aggrandizement, gratuitous socialization, naive humanism—into adulthood. Being creative in public is ugly decadence. It should be one's private practice. It is like shitting or masturbation. Part of life but secret. Unless you're really, really good, which almost no one is. Maybe I just don't understand, see certain people erroneously, from outside, with a submerged jealousy that registers as contempt. No, I don't think so. More than anything, it's just not enjoyable to talk to other people. Making friends is stupid. People who travel around to hang out make me sick. I don't want to see myself in others. I've never met anyone I found impressive or even interesting. Interesting people try to destroy the world, fail, and live in jail, or just never go out, live with Mom till age 100. I'm not impressive or interesting; if I ever met someone worthwhile, they rightly would fail to notice me. I had nothing to offer society. Maybe I would learn things in the future by trying and teaching myself things, and meet one or two good persons with whom I might talk about things and drink. In the short term, I wanted a job. That was all.

A week passed. My dad asked me again where I wanted to work.

"I want to knock down abandoned houses with a sledgehammer."

"You what?"

"I want to knock down houses with a sledgehammer. Demolition. Something like that. Involving waste."

I borrowed my dad's car and traveled to the edge of the city, an industrial area where no one lived. A wide highway with liquor stores, motels, refineries, various types of wholesalers or manufacturers, squat brick buildings in nondescript gray or beige. I drove up a hill, toward a public landfill I had found evocative in the past. A big expanse of multicolored garbage was strewn across a great horizon. Little orange vehicles slid around distantly, scooping up trash and dumping it out again. They seemed a new type of crab on some Martian beach, 3000 AD. More immediately, someone threw a filthy wooden bed frame over a ledge. It detonated into a plume of dust, as though rigged with explosives. Another little vehicle waited on the edge of the scene to move it away. It was like a premonition, the optimistic vision of a world to come. I wanted to interact with it, sift through layers.

To my right, birds watched a fat black guy in blue coveralls stack up air conditioners.

"Are you hiring?"

He laughed at that. I wasn't sure why. He pointed to a little trailer.

Inside, it was wood-paneled and seemed frozen in the 1970s. It smelled like fish and trash. An ugly old man drank coffee from a tiny Styrofoam cup.

"Are you hiring?"

He stayed fixed on the wall, seemingly in a dream.

"Are you hiring?"

He refused to speak. I was in the presence of some counter-elitism I've never conceived of. I earnestly regretted not being enough of a rude, repulsive failure to fit in. Then, panic. Maybe he really wasn't perceiving me.

"Can you see me?"

Now he looked at me. We shared a moment of mute fear, and I stumbled back into the glare, humiliated.

In front of a building down the street from the landfill, a plastic Fisher-Price whiteboard with the words NOW HIRING in magic marker. Inside, an enormous warehouse with trash bags stacked up to the ceiling. A Mexican guy drove a forklift that had been through a fire and was blackened on one side. There was a bright hole in the ceiling, water dripped in. It was kind of like the trash dump, but smaller and indoors.

"Are you hiring?"

Someone came out from behind a big green machine and took me to an office in the back. A white parrot was jumping around in a filthy cage. A Hispanic man explained that this is a clothing recycler. If that sounded OK, I could start tomorrow at ten dollars an hour.

In the kitchen I told Dad about my new job.

"Ten dollars an hour?" my dad said. "That's terrible."

I shrugged.

Dad was holding something in his right hand. A cheap black-and-white clock. The one we always had. Mom drank coffee under it every morning. It was one of the things we took.

"What's with the clock?"

"It stopped working."

"Can I keep it?" I said.

"Sure."

The first day they showed me what to do. You open up these bags. If the clothes are good, you put them in this bin. If the clothes are no good you put them in this bin. Good was something basically clean. Bad was something wet, moldy, stained, stored with rat shit. That stuff was getting shredded. Good clothes got thrown into a machine called a baler and turned into a golf cart–sized brick. Then that junk gets shipped overseas, allowing the third world to wear Bugle Boy and Rick and Morty tie-ins, as we, the enlightened, satisfy the ever-present need to stay "up to date."

"When the bins are full, roll them over here," the guy said, pointing to the locations where "good" and "bad" bins were to be rolled. Then I opened bags and made piles of clothes for eight hours. It was fine. Better than school, better than a lot of things.

That evening, I went on the computer and pirated audiobooks and put them on an mp3 player from 2008 I bought at a thrift store for $5.99. I made piles of clothes listening to Albert Camus, in English this time. I was done with French. When I quit things, I was really done. The first week, I listened to *The Stranger*, *The Fall*, then Sartre, *Nausea*. I found a setting to listen to the audiobooks at 1.5x speed. Trucks came and unloaded enormous boxes of clothing. Where did these come from? It didn't matter.

I saw some clothes I wanted in one bag then another, old items, some military issue things. I made a third pile for them, directly on the soot-covered floor. "Can I buy these?" The Hispanic guy I usually interfaced with looked around, like, no one's watching. You take them, OK, and he gave me a thumbs-up.

It was a good job. Mostly because it just sealed me in place and forced me to consume literature I otherwise would probably read sixty pages of then skim while juggling dozens of other random thoughts. Words have a structural quality on the page, the way they're physically arranged, that you lose when you listen to audiobooks, but otherwise it's very enjoyable.

They said I could work as much or little as I wanted. I worked from 8:00 AM to 3:30 PM, Monday through Thursday. I learned during this period I would be inheriting $137,000 from my mom's estate but I said my dad could just have it. Instead, he is going to put it in some fund for me or something. I don't want to know the details. I would like literally to burn it. I may give it to an animal charity, or maybe just an actual animal, drop it at its feet in a field. I can't think of anything I care about less than money. I don't want to make or use money, I don't want to seek money, I don't want to want money, it is an annoyance, a layer to things that shouldn't exist. I want the value of all money to hollow out, I wanted to see the US dollar become an empty signifier in my lifetime, a valueless token, spiritually bereft. Not in a liberal way or a right-wing way, I just think everything is going the wrong direction. I stared into the road and sorted the clothing. A shaft of light held dust motes like a snow globe. The wonderful desolate quality of these bags. You tore at them, they looked like a big fruit, or ovum, and the textiles spilled out. Sometimes it was just dirty rags. They pay me in cash here, which seems incredibly brazen, but the people are all illegal immigrants, so, it's just what they do.

I'm never going to file taxes. I'm never going to take out loans. I'm never going to establish credit. I have a driver's license, but I resent it. I would like to throw away my "Social Security Card" and forget the number, but I'd probably regret it, because, inescapably, I am a slave. All this Matrix, fake reality shit is repulsive. Do other people think about how ridiculous the way we're organized is? Our lives are fake and absurd. I would like to ignore that fake layer of things, the scam paperwork layer. That is the lowest layer, completely illusory and actually dangerous, a disaster. If I controlled the world that layer would be banned. Almost everyone would die, because this illusory human world that we built over the real one is just cancer. Markets and exchange with a manipulated representational token in the center, whose value is perversely molested, extracted through an algorithmic sleight of hand. The middle level is the physical, the real. Then there is the higher layer, the perfect opposite of the paperwork layer, religiosity, the secret realm, at war with the lowest level but completely subdued, subjugated in the modern world. But I hadn't effectively investigated that yet.

I started on a Thursday, so, at the end of the first full week they gave me $400 cash—plus I got to take home clothing. A Slipknot shirt, a Korn shirt, some baggy black jeans and cargo pants. There was a movie on TV over the weekend. It seemed like it was from the late '80s. Sometimes you think you've seen every interesting movie, then one surprises you. I felt really happy on that Sunday, sitting downstairs in the mildew-smelling basement, just wrapped up in blankets like someone dying of dementia and taking four doses of an almost expired bottle of Delsym cough syrup, just to blur the world a little and see my mind seeing my mind seeing my mind, the way weed did, but actually in the supreme manner of dextromethorphan, which I prefer to LSD, weed, kratom, Percocet, pretty much everything I've tried. Only Adderall I like better, but living through an amphetamine crash is too much like domestic trauma and submerging myself in bad memories. Plus I think it makes me dumb and gets me excited about my worst ideas.

It's more dangerous to fall in love with a drug that lies to you than it is even to die.

GIRL

During my second week at the job, I started going out for lunch. There is a gas station that sells chicken, so that's what it always smells like. I don't eat meat. Sometimes I do. It's wrong to eat meat, that's obvious, it's one of the only obvious things in the whole world, which is maybe why so few people notice it. But the way the system is set up, buying meat at the consumer level has no impact on the number of animals that are culled and is merely symbolic, a gesture. They don't even let you meaningfully extract yourself from the system. You think you're principled but it's already in everything you eat; dead animals line the roadway; you're stuck there on the bottom, subsidizing it. When I do eat meat, I consciously think, this is a depraved behavior, morally reckless, nihilistic to an extreme. Nothing else I do makes me feel that way. I am logical and think for myself. I am stupid but wise. I am like God in that way. Suicide is the only way out—mass murder, and genocide, all the better. Wading in the blood of your vanquished foes, carbon credits rain down like heavenly manna, a ticker tape parade. Poking at these thoughts, I noticed the cash register girl. She was staring at me.

I brought gummy worms and an energy drink to the counter.

"I like your shirt," she said.

It was a '90s shirt of Charles Manson. His face on the front, CHARLIE DON'T SURF on the back.

"Thanks."

"Bye!" she yelled as I left.

I turned to respond but I was outside and looking at myself. She was like the girl in *The Brown Bunny* that Vincent Gallo tries to kidnap. She had this frail and undersized, slightly inbred quality that was extremely erotic to me. I normally think of myself as pretty asexual, but extremely thin and genetically damaged looking women sometimes make me question myself.

She's trailer park runaway perfection. And I think she likes me . . .

EARLY LIFE

I lived in Brooklyn until I was eight years old. Of that period, I remember mostly the fighting between my mother and father, and the repulsive subway, and the oily sidewalk that smells like fish guts. Dad and I moved to Baltimore when they split up. They both were raised in Maryland, but Mom was more successful, so she stayed in New York. If you can hear me, tell me how that worked out for you? I'm really not mad. These little comments are my way of working through things.

From sixth to the end of tenth grade I had a best friend, Nick. We would just stay in the basement and watch TV. When I think of him, I remember the smell of the basement and the tasteless little items his parents decorated with. One day I didn't want to be friends any longer. I just didn't think he was at my level. There were things I wanted to say but they didn't make sense in the conversation. There wasn't room for growth in the space between us. It just didn't seem useful to continue spending time with him. I think it hurt him. I liked that. Not a ton, but it certainly didn't bother me. There was something satisfying in imagining people looking for me, and not being there, people saying, "What has come over him?" because you're not doing what they expect you to do. There is a slightly "heartrending" feeling in it.

Is that how my relationship with my new girlfriend would end? Just not be willing to see her anymore? No, I didn't think so. But it would end, because these things usually do. . . . It's like death, no one spends a ton of time thinking about it, but it's really the only story that counts. Why be present in a relationship when something will come between? It is like hanging a painting you know is a forgery and will later take down. This is what normal people did. That was the reason why I was doing it. I was trying to be normal, slightly. I would see her this weekend for the third time.

Something bad was coming.

The only real question was, how heartrending would it be?

CAR

After a month of working at the textile recycler, my dad bought me a car, mostly because he was tired of dropping me off and picking me up. I chose the car, selecting an old Subaru station wagon, the classic lesbian Green Party car; it made me think of aughts leftism, the last time the left was tolerable—the only car more beautiful than that is the discontinued Ford Crown Victoria, but a Crown Vic is unrealistic, also somewhat depressing and reminds me too much of black squalor, which Baltimore already overloads you with as it is.

I liked my job and I took a lot of clothes home. The Hispanic people didn't really talk to me and I just listened to audiobooks. In a certain way, this was college but tolerable.

I ran into the girl from the gas station at a thrift store.

"Hey, didn't you used to work at the gas station?"

I hadn't seen her there in a while. I went in all the time.

"I was fired for missing work."

She was wearing vaguely goth clothes, but hillbilly too. She was really a winner. Too bad I'm too shitty at life to say anything.

"Oh," I said. "See you."

I went back two days later and there she was again.

I leaned into a bin. This was a store called an outlet store, with shittier, cheaper clothing that you pull out of bins. She stood opposite me. Her forearm, with downy blond hair, would sometimes brush against mine. "I'm going to a show this weekend if you want to go," she said.

"OK," I said. Then I caught myself, "I can't. I don't have a phone."

"Do you want to just meet up here at eight on Saturday?"

"Oh, OK."

For the next two days, when I would think about Saturday, I got an MDMA-like feeling—a sort of tingling on my scalp. Is that "liking" someone? The human body is a weird garbage dump, with many secret pockets of gas and sludge.

DATE

I got to the store at like 7:45.
 Maybe she just wanted a ride or something. I thought, I can still get out of this. She walked up to me and gave me a shy look, like not really looking up. I saw the future. She would be my girlfriend, for at least a little while. But she wasn't the story here, and would never be. I don't feel love. Sex is no big deal at best, and romance is a massive joke.

In fact, I didn't like the destabilized, nervous feeling I was experiencing. I had an impulse to say something like, "I changed my mind" and drive home—but that's dumb, right? It didn't really matter. Nothing mattered. The scenario laid out before me was a bit like how I saw my life, I was here despite everything; I should probably just see it through. Plus, maybe I could get something practical out of it.

With that, the answer arrived.

It wouldn't be heartrending at all.

THE MAN WHO REFUSED

"I'm dead already," the man in bed said. "Nothing matters anymore." Downstairs, his daughter was walking around their dirty town house in Parkville, Maryland, a lower-middle-class suburb of Baltimore County, not far from the city line. His wife was standing in the bedroom doorway. "I'm refusing to do everything," he said.

"You're what?" she said.

"I'm already dead."

It was 2017. Donald Trump had surprised America by being elected president. *Star Wars: The Last Jedi* was the year's most successful movie. Things in America were changing, but in other ways they were staying the same. The man in bed was one of the things changing, but also staying the same.

"I'm not doing anything anymore. I'm no longer responsible for anything. If you need a divorce, fine."

He was having a bad day. She closed the door. He did this a year earlier, stayed in bed all day because he was depressed. He needs to stop doing this. If he needs to talk to someone, that's fine. But he can't miss work for bullshit like this.

The young girl went to school and her mother went to work. When they came back, he was still in bed. It was dark outside. The mother and daughter ate dinner together, watched TV. The mother fell asleep on the couch. The big-screen TV ran all night, made the room glow blue, like an aquarium. The venetian blinds were drawn, but broken in places, as though voyeuristic ghosts were fingering them and peering inside. The neighborhood was neither good nor bad, somewhere in the middle, and going in the wrong direction. The daughter slept in her room. The father slept in the bed.

He did it again the next day. "I'm not getting up." He had stopped doing everything, like he said he would, and their life began to fall apart, gradually at first and without a great deal of heightened emotion.

"I just can't. I literally am unable." He muttered these statements to himself and turned over in bed. His work called during the first day he missed, then the second day. On the fourth day they called for a final time. He deleted the voicemails without listening.

The father slept during the day and would wander downstairs to get food in the night. The weekend came and he stayed in bed. His wife stopped talking to him. Sometimes when the house was quiet, he would drink in the morning, but he wasn't an alcoholic. He merely wanted to change some of the thoughts he was having.

Two weeks into the era of refusal he moved to the couch to let his wife have the bed. It seemed "only right." Then it was awkward with his wife walking by all the time and sitting there angrily watching shows all night. He went into the basement and slept on a sleeping bag next to the washing machine. Eventually he ordered an air mattress from the internet. When that started deflating, he ordered a regular mattress.

There was a photograph on the wall taken in either 2014 or 2015. It was still up in 2024. It shows three people sitting together on a deck. A husband, his wife, and their daughter. It was taken by the brother of the woman in the photograph. They looked happy. That's why it was on the wall.

Later it became obvious that they had never been happy. Least of all, the man. A year into the man's total refusal to uphold his responsibilities, his wife found a new boyfriend. His name is Wayne, and he knew her husband. They went to middle school together. Wayne has never stayed overnight, given everything . . .

There was a brief period when the husband didn't live in the basement. He stayed at Airbnbs. His wife was extremely mad at him, and even though she had stopped speaking when he was in the room, the rage she radiated was unendurable. He felt it was better to be away, even if he died.

He walked in one day to get something. He had a black eye, all purple and blue on one side of his face.

"What happened?"

"What?"

"Someone hit you?"

"My black eye? I got it all alone, honest to God, without even moving," he said.

His wife opened her mouth. Fear welled up, then disgust. "I don't know what the fuck happened to you and, actually, you know what, I don't fucking care," she said, walking away. A memory of their wedding, the way certain pictures come back unexpectedly. The stained glass reflected in his eyes was like cartoon sunken treasure—rubies. Now the red was blood because the man was dying? She was letting him die because his brain was malfunctioning. He is a broken animal. A man with problems is just an animal that is worn out, she realized, jolted by this objective glimpse of man's condition, washed of social conditioning. A man in distress is not a bad person. He is more like a sickly farm animal moaning and thrashing. She turned around, panicked.

"I care," she said, stomping down the steps. "I'm sorry I said I don't care."

He had gotten what he needed and was gone.

The mother and daughter sat mutely, just waiting to hear the man died. The house took on characteristics of a haunting: blackly shadowed rooms, a smoky smell, some high-pitched feedback sound no one could find or fix. The sickness had jumped from them to the inanimate house, like if one can imagine a blight that survives in deer, then trees.

This poltergeist-like family problem was driving the young daughter insane. Instead of wearing mall clothes, bright and positive colors, her look became gothic, exaggerated and ironic, lace and flames—dirty items, torn in places, like Snow White after wandering through the haunted forest.

The father got arrested. He had been sleeping in the car or something, drinking in a parking lot. He moved back in, was permitted to reside in the basement, basically safe, but out of sight, until he figured things out.

At this time, and in a decidedly limited way, they became a family again.

Should a fucked-up family exist, or should it be dissolved?

Is it good they let weakness bring them back together?

Should they have found the strength to truly, and permanently, be pulled apart?

The family I am describing never should have existed.
Their lives were a mistake, the union a mistake, the child a mistake. When you think of some people as being one in a million, they are the opposite. They are superfluous. The founding couple are two dismal, depressing people, who not only lack joy but all insight into their condition.
This was a family that was better off dead. They should have lit the house on fire, and gripped the chairs they sat in, on a trip to whatever's next, like someone on a carnival ride. What then was left of their lives together amounted to some fiscal concerns, various appointments, giving rides to the man, legal obligations, largely relating to the father's precarious disability status.
The curtains glow like urine on a T-shirt. The light comes in now. The room is bright. Outside, flowers grow in an accelerated way and a bluebird lands on a fence. Things have stabilized somewhat after several turbulent years, and they walk a golden path as a family, seeing things from inside out, and over again.
It's really beautiful to see the sun again, though it stings my eyes a little. The way our lives came back together, or not. Give me a minute. I'm not sure . . .
I'm really lonely now and missing you. I think I am sorry again for what I did when we messed everything up, the man said, and walked a trail, under pylons.

*

I am dating the daughter in this story. Her name is Grace, but she goes by Dill, which is what her mother called her as a kid.

I was thinking about writing a book about Dill and her family, even though I don't know how to write at all. What would that even be like? Maybe feature eerie photographs of the family doing ordinary tasks—but something missing, something not lining up—and just describing their lives in a flat way, all this banality and pointlessness that adds up to horror when stacked high enough. I think my dad may help me. Then I won't have to process clothes for the rest of my life. But I'm not sure a book like that would make sense to anyone. Does anything like that even exist?

I can make people like it. It should be dark, but then become lighter, I decide, letting the images bloom in my imagining—the despair in the house with stained walls, then light in a window (an almost religious image), and the man under pylons like skeletons of giants; then he is small; then he is gone. The images dissipated as I shifted my attention to driving. I put in a Chopin CD—crystalline pings, like dropped ice, the feeling of it. At a red light I squinted.

The world is a mystery.

The world is a blur.

GIRLFRIEND

Dill and I have been together for three months. On our first date we went to a party in Timonium—an upper-middle-class suburb, north of the city.

She knew the kids who were having it. She called it a show. It was a small and chaotic party, with this really bad band playing in the basement in front of the TV and becoming out of control and punching the family portrait and knocking over vases, which I loved and found hilarious—and beautiful? I was having fun actually, which surprised me.

The police were called, and we ran out a back door and through another backyard—it was very dark and autumn. Someone was having a fire somewhere, you could smell it. We emerged on some suburban road, and it was only 10 or so, but it felt later, or like some secret time, where everyone vanishes for five minutes as God moves things around like someone playing chess. All the houses seemed empty, like we could just walk in and yell "is anyone home" into an echoing abyss . . .

We moved to the sidewalk and nervously mimicked extreme normalcy, walking with faux-stiffness, like a self-consciously professional man on his first day at a new job, chuckling a bit, letting any sound shrink behind us. We found the car and drove around carefully, worried about getting pulled over. There was a romantic feeling then, revealing beauty in tension and evasion. We drove to a grocery store open twenty-four hours and took seats at the glossy, empty tables.

"Do you know about the Browning Family Murders?" she asked.

"No, what's that?"

"A preppy kid killed his family in the 2000s."

"Do you want to hear something interesting about me?" I asked.

"Sure."

"My mom was murdered last June."

"What happened?"

"Someone killed her."

"What?!" She looked shocked, amazed.

"I don't want to be rude, but can we change the subject?"

"Hey, this area is closed," some guy said, I think lying.

"I should take you back," I said. She didn't say anything. I could tell she was still thinking about my mother, and me in this context—a boy whose mother was murdered.

I treated anything related to my mother's death like an eclipse. I let the light in, a bit, but wasn't able to look directly at the event. In preparation for dealing with my mother's death, I was beginning to become interested in her life.

SEX LIVES

I left New York with my dad when I was ten. They screamed insanely when I was eight and nine. I remember my mother called my dad jealous of her. She was more successful, though he never seemed jealous. I thought it was a mean thing to say. I was going to doctors—a therapist, a psychiatrist. One did tests. He said I was smart, but with abnormalities? Possible autism spectrum disorder. Then when I was ten, they stopped all the yelling and turmoil—it was like sun after a storm, so pronounced and different—only to sit me down and in this very formal, very rehearsed-seeming way, tell me they would be divorcing, and that they didn't have money to rent two apartments in New York, and that your dad would be moving back to Baltimore; first he will be moving in with your grandmother, then he will probably be buying a house, and they wanted to know who I would rather be with.

"I want to go with Dad," I said. That was the expected response. They seemed to be guiding me that way with all the talk about Baltimore. They knew I didn't mind visiting my grandmother. Her house was comfortable, even though she always seemed kind of unknowable, distant, like someone from a different world than me. There was a kid in those days who lived in the same building in New York. Elliot something. They made us hang out that one time. It was awful. Then we gave each other these looks in the hallway. He hated me and I was basically frightened of him. He was a black kid, but it wasn't about that. It was kind of a class divide, or culture divide, or something. He had his friends, I had my friends. Even at ten there was this tension. There were more things about New York I wanted to get away from than hold on to. I wanted to live somewhere like we would visit when we were on vacation, the beach or a national park—something like that, but that was unrealistic, I guess. My dad and I moved in with my grandmother in the suburbs. I got a bunch of new video games and a tablet. I think they wanted me to get lost in screens to forget how fucked they made everything, I poked around in the basement, found old photos. I think in that time I developed an interest in old things. My dad's dad was a conservative, somewhat eccentric man. I never met him, but apparently I would have liked him. He died before I was born.

    I talked to my mom a lot on the phone, particularly the first few months. That period had a tragic feeling, like a song about memories, or the final line of an emotional book. I still remember the strange atmosphere of it. It was like being in a sad movie. I started fifth grade. Then, in a flash, as fast as a dream, I was in middle school. During those summers, I would spend a few weeks with her. She took me to Indian restaurants I liked, movie theatres, the Nintendo store—the New York things I had a positive view of. I got the sense she was trying to "spoil" me so to avoid feeling ashamed, kind of buying me off. In a deeper way our relationship became distant. It was like spending time with a generous, rich aunt more so than a mother. My grandmother died of cancer. It happened one year when I was away. That was another sad time, though the relationship I had with her wasn't that meaningful to me.

When I got back at the end of that summer, her bed was gone, and the house was different. When people are gone, they're really gone. They never stop by for visits anymore. Life is so sad it should make us all insane. We stayed in that house a few more years so I could continue to attend the same middle school in the county, then before high school my dad bought a town house in the city, and I started going to private school.

In those days, I wanted to be a writer like my parents. One afternoon, I googled my mother to read more of her writing. The first link was an op-ed she wrote about her open marriage. Open marriage—what even is that? The phrase kind of stunned me, despite not really understanding. I knew it was something bad, something "disturbing."

People talk about where they were when something traumatic happened—I really do remember everything about that moment. I had a bottle of water next to the keyboard. The sky was blue outside the window. My mother wrote this in *The Guardian*. This was all public information? Who knew about this? It was an excerpt from her memoir—why had my mother written a memoir? She never told me about this. I thought I knew about her books, but they had hidden this from me. My family had these secrets, but they also weren't secrets—it was all very odd. My mother's book was called *Sex Lives*. *Sex Lives*? My mother wrote a book called *Sex Lives*? And it was about her life?

I used to like going to bookstores, then I developed this anxiety that I would run into the book. I didn't know what the book looked like, so I imagined it as a close-up picture of my mother's face, sometimes with glazed eyes, like she had been crying. I envisioned a stack of the books, with one standing vertically atop the pile, exactly my height. Eye to eye with my mother, reading the caption, *Sex Lives*, and her name. Maybe the other people in the store understood, knew my mother's book, knew who I was. It didn't seem far-fetched. In fact, it was a very vivid and disturbing image that caused me to avoid bookstores and libraries. This book I hadn't read created invasive thoughts. Had my teachers read it? The book was about my parents' "open marriage," but I guess it also talked about me, because it was all about her life, right? Did people read this book and wonder how much I knew? Did people read this book and think my family was perverted? Maybe they thought I was having sex too. I was just a small child. I had no interest in that. I felt dragged into something horrifying. It gave me a feeling like—well, like if someone had kidnapped my pet, and called me to tell me they were torturing it, and you could hear it crying in the background. When I looked at the computer, I felt tension. It was like a doorway to horror, or a flipped-over photograph of something gory. You're looking at the back of the photograph, wanting to turn it over, wanting to see the bloody image, but also not, and this feeling creating tension—excitement? It was an energizing feeling, but it also ruined my appetite. I remember crying, not wanting to eat much for a few days.

The word "jealous" came back when I realized it had two meanings. All their fights. You're jealous! Was she talking about having sex with other men? I think I realized how self-interested everyone is then. I began to hate. I hated my mother. I hated society. I hated biology. I hated the idea of these impulses. I didn't want to be an adult. I didn't want to have sex, but apparently I would one day? That seemed evil to me. Like an alien force kidnapping my mind and making me want something dark, losing control and doing things against my will, just to silence some pestering voice, like schizophrenics instructed to drive off a cliff or burn their own house down. That was my concept of sexuality—it was also the bleak reality I was wandering toward, no chance of escape. It sounds strange now, but in those days, I was thinking about castration. It was an idea I was interested in. I separated myself from society. I became, in my own, odd way, somewhat philosophical—I started questioning basic precepts about life and society, wondering why people did the things they did, wondering if I would do the things they did. I even started thinking about killing people. Not like I was actually going to do it, or like I had any real drive in that direction, but I just felt so radically different, and this feeling of not belonging turned to hate, manifesting in these flashes of mass murder, mass casualty events. Like images that I barely participated in but that I oversaw, and approved of? Walking past bloodied bodies in a silver building made out of metal. The dead people looked like discarded puppets, their legs and arms bent strangely. I imagined a big freezer and all these blue figures, camouflaged against the icy walls. I imagined an ocean with dozens of floating bodies, the backs of people who had drowned, and the sun rising over it and the whole world turning orange. A green field, like Ireland, or a screensaver, and these dried bodies, all nude, that looked shriveled and dark, like prunes, or a type of mushroom, barely human at all. I kicked one and it exploded into dust.

*

"Tell Mom I don't want to talk to her anymore."
"What?"

"I want you to tell your ex-wife that I don't want to talk to her anymore."

I was twelve or thirteen.

He refused to say it to her. If I wanted to change my relationship with my mother, I would have to explain it to her. So I did. With some relish, I said over the phone, "I decided I don't like you and don't want to see you anymore."

"Armand, what? Why are you saying this? Put your dad on the phone."

He explained that he didn't know what it was all about, and that he hated it, thought it was terrible of me to say that. I listened to them, enjoying something about this.

My dad took me to a psychiatrist. I didn't say anything about my mom's book—it would have been impossible; I had an extreme pathological aversion to the book—and instead explained in a very logical and considered-seeming way that my mother's choices were the reason why my family broke up, and I felt she was a selfish person who had harmed me.

The psychiatrist said, "You are very mature for your age."

My dad talked to him privately. On the way home, my dad said that if I didn't want to talk to my mother anymore, he couldn't make me, but he hoped I would reconsider. I said I would think about it.

Eventually she stopped trying to reach me, but apparently stayed in contact with my dad and he let her know how I was doing. On my birthdays, and on Christmas she sent me money and folded-up letters that seemed long but that I didn't read. I imagined her tears landing on the paper and exploding like water balloons. Every once in a while we spoke. I felt that we both had moved on. She made choices that caused me to act this way.

I enjoyed meting out this punishment and enforcing rules.

FRIDAY

I had a birthday. Nineteen years old. I kept going to the job. I usually hang out with Dill on Fridays. Tonight, the first Friday of December, I picked her up at like seven.

I waited in my car for her to come out. There were rags of snow around. They punctuated the dark world with little mounds resembling dead poodles. It was warm and starting to rain. 7 PM had a midnight look; Christmas lights hung haloed in the dark air.

*

Dill lives in a small town house. Something about the fact that she's poor, something about the fact that she's from a less-cultured background makes me like her more. My family, like Dill's family, was a failure. It never should have existed. We both were by-products of failed unions, misshapen fruit from the tree of regret. These details make her sympathetic to me. Also, I feel like they don't judge me for not going to college. I'm insecure about that fact, and uncomfortable if it comes up in conversation. I am glad I'm not in college, but I feel like other people don't understand and probably just think it means I'm even dumber than most people, or a failure already, someone doomed to "flip burgers" and live in penury.

I sometimes think about what that "wagie" life would be like, compared to what my parents experienced. It doesn't seem worse. My parents were extremely ambitious, even though I think they preferred to seem like arty or "punk" parents who don't care about things and just live life, man. I have realized that the people who present as being creative and carefree are often the most driven and status-obsessed, so much so that they develop a careful persona that kind of makes people think the opposite, a complicated diversionary tactic—or at the very least indicating a fealty to surfaces, and presentation as idiot communication. I remember the excitement in our household when I was small and my mother was getting new professional opportunities. We went on the subway all the time, ate out all the time, met all sorts of people. My mother was constantly introducing me to people, people I could tell I was supposed to be impressed by, or at least that my parents were impressed by, but that I knew, even then, were just bullshitters and people who treated society like a video game. They were worse actually than everyone else; they had a sickness that made them very sensitive to status signifiers and a lot of other strange, and in a certain way, very tragic materials that people trade in to become socially mobile in America. If they let go of the game they would probably be better, happier people, but the idea was unthinkable, and maybe impossible even to conceive of.

I have imagined a life like this: I work 24-32 hours a week and live in a small apartment. I have a job that's extremely easy and I am invisible. I can listen to audiobooks all day and just stay in my own little world, as meaningless things happen all around me. I have a girlfriend but I don't see her much. We have sex just so often that I don't think about sex. Sometimes we go to the movies when a new movie comes out that we both want to see. Otherwise I am mostly left alone, with some books and video games and interesting objects I like looking at and living with. Nothing ever happens, but sometimes I work on writing. Maybe the world outside the room is not even real, it changes spontaneously, all the time. But I'm locked away and safe from it, like a hunchback in the belfry. The way I see it, it would be paradise.

*

Dill walks outside.

She stands under the porch light for a minute and waves at me to come in.

I turn the car off and walk toward their little house.

"Nice to see you," she says.

"Nice to see you," I say.

She hugs me and we go inside. She really is a very attractive person, I think as we move from the purple and dark outside-world to the butter-yellow and extremely bright inside-world of her mother's house. I guess it is her parents' house. They both live here, but I think of it as her mother's house. Her father is really a strange case, somewhat interesting to me though.

"Hey sit down a minute," she says. "I'll be ready in a second."

I go through the applications on the TV, streaming services—Netflix, Amazon Prime. I watch five minutes of a movie called *Angst* I like on their big screen TV, then Dill comes downstairs, wearing gothic clothes, but that seem like the past, like someone in a smeared Polaroid from thirty years ago.

MOTHER

My mother was a feminist. She critiqued society by taking a basically benign image and finding some flaw in it by way of viewing it through a lens. In a certain way I continued this project but in a more radical and total way, albeit completely private and with no practical application.

I was always in my own little world, not paying attention to the people around me. Now my mother is gone, and I don't know anything about her. These are the things I know . . .

When I was young, I thought her behavior was normal. In families, even the most heinous behavior has the feeling of normalcy, it is the water you breathe, the air you swim in, the other way around, but you know what I mean. The water you breathe.

I remember being seven years old. Maybe eight. I walked up to her to hold her leg—I was frightened by something—and she pushed me away, held me at arm's length as I robotically swam toward her, my arms and legs moving frantically but going nowhere, like a dumb robot grinding against a wall.

Did I make this up? Where were we? I remember a green bush, like a hedge maze. Are memories that old even reliable, or just as likely a fabrication, derived from something observed in a movie, or experienced in a dream. I remember it as abuse or neglect, but she must have had a reason, right? The image has no moral heft; it is merely confusing.

Think of someone you know who died, someone from your distant past—as distant as your past can go, a stubby cave in my case, but still murky in its shallow recesses. How concrete do the memories seem? If someone told you with some authority that those events never occurred, that the characterization you retain of a vanished person is a distortion, how easily might you believe them? Now think of someone from even longer ago. How real are they in your memory? Are they solid at all?

I haven't seen my mother in five years—actually longer—and I will never see her again. The distance between us will only grow, the memories becoming blurry and protean, like snapshots seen through gel—expired lubricant in a medicine cabinet, flaky and discolored.

When a child is born, what obligations begin? Are you required to maintain a clean home, a standard of upkeep? Should you give up weird sex behaviors, or just keep them completely secret? If the child fails, where does the blame lay?

I am trying to remember my mother. I would like to write about her, but I don't feel anything. She went on a book tour in 2016. She was assaulted when she was fourteen, that break-in she wrote an essay about, what else . . .

Her favorite book was a novel called *Speedboat* by Renata Adler. She would only read women writers. (I always found that tacky—like a fake daring pose. "I only read women writers. Please clap.") She wore black. She tried to maintain an artistic appearance. She pretended to be indifferent to appearances but was very interested in her own appearance. She got a facelift, something like that, some kind of procedure to have the skin around her chin pulled more tightly.

I remember the bandages, and the straw-like tubes for draining.

ASSAULT

On July 3, 1992, two teenage boys broke into my grandparents' house in Glen Arm, Maryland. They emerged from the woods like the villains in a fable. They were sixteen and seventeen years old.

My mother grew up in a modernist A-frame house designed by her father, a psychiatrist associated with Johns Hopkins and a very cultured man. He wrote several books, and died on New Years Day, 2000. A fact my mother told me when I was a kid and always found memorable, as though he was truly a person of the past, unable to exist in the harsh air of true modernity. In our apartment in New York there were many photographs of the house she grew up in. I remember almost wine-red floorboards and threadbare Persian rugs, rows of books, and curious sculptures, masks, paintings, from their many interesting travels. The photographs were taken more recently, but in my remembering, they have the highly saturated quality of a film or postcard snapshot from the 1950s—infecting all my memories of my mother's upbringing with a lovely dreaminess, even when the facts of her life become dark.

My grandfather and grandmother visited the Big Sur area during their honeymoon. When they returned to the East Coast as a young couple, they wanted to to create a home that conveyed the same quality of warmth, closeness to nature, and rustic elegance as the homes they saw there. In this effort they were successful, as photographs of the house, I have seen—and even in the real estate listings I investigated and researched—there is a feeling of bohemia, but also affluence, a kind of good taste that is instinctive and hard to fake.

They bought a heavily forested plot of land near the reservoir, very dark and damp with moss and ferns. In pictures, it looked lush and enchanted. It seemed a lovely place.

The Charles H. Hickey Jr. School was opened in 1855, then called The House of Refuge. It was a juvenile detention facility, "juvie," essentially jail. Though different than a prison in that it served children; as such, its purpose, in the writings of its first president, was to reform and educate, and not to punish. The location was consciously chosen and bordered a lush forest so to offer "the wayward lads of the city" some bucolic alternative. It didn't work. Suicide by hanging was common. The *Baltimore Sun* wrote, "the dominant problem at the school was fear.' Inmates run away out of fear. Many guards fear for their lives." Superintendent Dr. Charles Leas whipped the children and subjected them to punishments of "unnecessary and injudicious severity." Boys escaped frequently, often in large groups. They even sometimes died in their frenzy to leave, such as in 1898 when a young man "either jumped or fell" from a fourth-story window.

I read my mom's essay, "A Theory of the Break-In," in my dad's copy of her first collection of linked essays, titled *Studies*. The blurbs on the back of the book called it masterful and "Foucauldian." Only one essay referred to her sex life—it was oriented around discomfort instead of pleasure, which made it nontraumatic to read. I became interested in the Hickey school. It seemed like a place of great suffering. I imagined it like something the Marquis de Sade might have invented. Boys lined up in a white room, whipped and branded. My mother seemed interested in it too, and included in the piece part of a letter a boy from Hickey sent the *Baltimore Sun* in 1908:

> When a fellow has no mother and no one to love him or sympathize with him or to teach him, it's mighty hard to be put into an institution and beaten often when he doesn't deserve it. We are full of life when it's not taken out of us and mischievous, but not one of us is criminally inclined unless we're made so and that is not our fault. Be gentle and kind to us; let us feel that you are our friend and love us and want to help us, and you will soon find that you can win us and we will honor and love and obey you.

Decades passed; the summer of 1992 arrived. My mother was fourteen years old. Her parents were in their mid-fifties. Her mother was forty-one when she had her, pushing a child through the doorway of her body just before nature forbade it. They were away from home that day. I imagine the perspective of the two escapees: just as I walked through the woods during my vacation with my father, they had wandered a long time, away from the school, hungry, and thirsty—it was hot—they grew agitated, they hid in the woods, came to a house, triangular, unlike any house they had known, like the domicile of elves, or an elaborate tree fort, something constructed by a genius child . . .

What did they see when they ran up that hill? When did they see my mother? They caught her in the backyard. There was a deck. In the essay she said she was sunbathing. She had her swimsuit on. She looked like something God was providing them—a child offering. One boy tackled her. She was small as a woman, certainly smaller still at fourteen. She probably screamed, maybe into the lawn, her face pressed into the grass, one of the boys sitting on her back, like a sick parody of sibling turmoil. If I were the boys, if I had been stuck in a place like that, maybe for something I didn't even do, and saw someone small, someone I could hurt, who knows . . .

They were wearing their blue prison uniforms. CHARLES HICKEY SCHOOL FOR BOYS stenciled on the back. It was in the '90s, but for some reason the scene my mind renders is of the late '60s, early '70s—the era of Woodstock, race riots, Vietnam, Charles Manson, man on the moon. My grandfather's house seemed a little out of time. Maybe that was it. Maybe it blurred with all the movies about rape I've watched from that period. *The Last House on The Left—I Spit On Your Grave—They Call Her One-Eye.* They are very beautiful movies, all evoking dank forests—the loneliness and danger of such locations, not the innate dangers of forests but the way man is altered by that environment, concealed and then intoxicated by it.

One boy grabbed her arms, the other grabbed her legs. They carried her toward the house. She was dangling like a '70s smiley face smile, the boys her two eyes. No adults around. She was all alone. One boy dropped her. The other boy held tight to her wrists, dragged her over the deck slats, splinters raising and sticking into her, the cracking sound of a bonfire. The boy who dropped her slid the glass deck door open. Inside the house it was cool and dark, the house was always dark. These modern comforts, everything arranged so perfectly, the way people create a monument to their own good taste, as though they're not fully sure, making sure they know, and willing to go broke to prove it.

The records, tastefully chosen. Jazz—Dave Brubek, Miles Davis. The art on the wall. The young girl screaming in the beautiful house. Summer vacation. Framed Matisse poster. I know the photographs I saw were from before the attack. No one took photographs after. They moved after all this, of course. Events change a house. My parents had their horrible fights. It was nice to be able to leave.

"A Theory of the Break-In" was written in 2008. It described this event, then even more violent crimes she researched. It was very popular on feminist blogs of the period, in those days, when online feminism was an ascendant force, a vanguard ideology, before I'm With Her, 2016, and soap commercials that parodied Dionysian atmospheres with fat black "bodies." She wrote beautifully about the attack by the two boys who escaped from the Charles Hickey School. Near the end of the piece, like many writers of "theory," she mistook metaphor and simile for psychological insight and declared, in a very general sense, *men break into things*. They break into conversations. They break into houses. They break into women's bodies. It begins at the earliest, on playgrounds they break into women's games, throw dirt on their faces. The essay was about the way men are taught to break into things . . .

One boy knocked over random items in the kitchen, the blender, the toaster, the coffeepot. Bang! Crash! Boom! I imagine sound balloons, like from a comic book, my mother splayed on the carpet, bleeding, splinters sticking out of her almost bare ass. Hey, bitch. Hey bitch—wake up bitch. I'm awake, she responded. They pulled down her bikini top, she was so young then, between a girl and a woman. Maybe they slapped her. Her cheek changed color like a mood ring. A dot of blood on her lips. My mother in agony. Shortly thereafter it ends. I wish I had some big violent rape to render, but I don't. That was it. They knocked some stuff over, dragged her around, mussed her hair a little, and left.

Now I'm standing over her. The front door is open, letting in the sounds of bugs and birds. Nature is *clicking* like something falling down a well, breaking through layers of paper. She's panting. The boys left the house. *I'm with her.* My mother is in the beautiful house with me now.

Relevant to the story of my mother's life was the feminist moment in culture. Mostly an online phenomenon, but I guess it spilled into the real world at times. If you remember. Which is to say, if you can extract that particular memory from all the political information Americans, maybe English-speakers more generally, were forced to bathe in, over the course of an eight-year period lasting, say, from 2013–2021.

That was a period of heightened civilizational drama—right? It seemed so at the time, but I also get the sense that these things are hard to quantify or sometimes illusory. That anxiety of it all is over now, I think. What was it? Well, it was many things. It was, in a very concrete way, the pandemic, and lockdown—a wonderful time, though I think it contributed to my eleventh grade breakdown—and the election of Donald Trump—I remember one of my teachers crying, and the kids looking around like aren't adults completely bizarre? It was more generally a time of enormous interest in politics—identity stuff, stuff I was always on the other side of, but tried not to be excessively on the other side of, sensing that was a cliff some people fall off of.

I did a lot of research about "identity politics" for my YouTube channel. When other kids were doing their homework, I was researching the history of third-wave feminism, and talking about "SJWs" with online weirdos—I thought the people I was talking to were like me, my age, et cetera, but in retrospect, there was no reason really to believe that at all. They could have been anyone. Some were probably very strange individuals. Was I a bored teenager online, looking for amusing, slightly naughty stuff, or was I one of those irreparably damaged people who felt most at home with images of hate? I would say, I was somehow both. Maybe like most everyone in that space.

The feminist wing of the weird politics epoch involved these dubious concepts developed in gender studies departments: the wage gap, rape culture, laments about the relative scarcity of women in STEM. It was Jessica Valenti, Everyday Feminism, Salon-dot-com, pussy hats. It was that very brief period of time when think pieces were a top performing unit of cultural and economic exchange, and clickbait mills like Vice and BuzzFeed looked like rising multinationals.

I easily discovered how fake it all was. First, the academic interest in the topic, which began in the early '70s in response to grassroots opposition to Vietnam in an effort to corral and neuter the left—CIA money, administered by foundations, were the seed funds for women's studies departments and cultural organs like *Ms.* magazine. And for decades these really dumb people, like high-functioning retarded people like Catharine MacKinnon, and Bell Hooks (oh, sorry, "bell hooks") released "papers" and presented their opinions about men and women as actual research, very serious business, and no one really cared, the whole thing was wasteful and nakedly absurd but benign, because the universe was a closed loop of journals no one read and thinkers no one thought about and that no organic market supported but that someone, or some number of people, associated with that seat of power known as the Western academy thought had some meaning or utility, and so it continued.

Then in about 2012, all this worthless froth floating in the informational ether skyrocketed in value—like a common mineral long overlooked, but newly useful in the production of microprocessors—and everyone started talking about rape culture, the glass ceiling, the patriarchy, and all these ideas that were neither particularly new nor particularly interesting. Why then? What happened? The same thing that happened to other academic ideas about race and gender. An event that seemed political was merely economic—industrial trolling garnering clickthroughs by the tonnage.

In 2014, *The Columbia Journalism Review* published an article titled "Stop Trolling Your Readers," with the byline: We know you're only doing it for clicks. The piece critiqued the media model characterized by headlines like "Are Men Really Necessary?," and "Yes, White People Are a Danger To Civilization." This "deliberate trolling," described by the writer as the "calculated decision to offend, anger, or appall publications' target readership" defined online discourse and American culture wars during the mid-2010s. It's well known that anger was the emotion that was found to most influence clicking, sharing, and commenting behaviors. Essays that presented as good-faith op-eds were in fact raw meat for chained up dogs to lunge at and fight over, even if many of the authors never realized they were being used this way. As Ben Smith, former editor-in-chief of BuzzFeed, wrote in his account of the period, "in the end, it was that same emotional substance that paid the bills and powered a decade of unrest."

Merging decades-old academic theory and angry emotionality was a dark art. It had to maintain a straight face, even during its most ridiculous permutations. The shortsighted impulse to chase virality inspired faithful adherents, but also backlash in the form of a virulent new right, a movement with, at times, an intriguing and apocalyptic aura. It exacerbated alienation and damaged trust in media. It drove vast amounts of traffic to niche blogs and inspired millions of comments, but also populist insurgencies like Black Lives Matter on the left and Trumpism on the right. These apparently spontaneous social movements were in fact massaged out of a population whose relationship to social media and the internet changed during years of surging smartphone adoption. Eventually everyone suffered—BuzzFeed, Vice and many outlets most associated with these behaviors failed, in part, as a result. The era was a catastrophe—social, cultural, ethical—though some successes emerged, some fortunes made.

My mother was among the beneficiaries of the period. She went from running a niche blog, to writing pieces that ran in *Salon*, then *The Guardian* and *The Atlantic*. Some of the opportunities dried up, but she had had her moment. Her mental health got worse, and her family fell apart, but I think the fact that she even briefly got the attention of the corporate media and individuals associated with the Atlantic Council, the Brookings Institution, and the Council on Foreign Relations made her life feel redeemed. She published books that otherwise would never have been released, and despite a very anti-establishment pose, having the attention of government-linked state media services made her feel very important and distinguished. Hippie people once had this fear of "selling out"—or maybe that was Gen X. Whatever that was, it was over by the time my mother found success. Leftists published on blogs owned by hedge funds. They posed as revolutionaries but worked—albeit in a vaguely convoluted, shell game–like way—for the national security state. It was all very absurd, frustratingly so—which is why people like me (a secret, subterranean elite) risked much to mock it.

I thought I would have my period of rebellion, then be rehabilitated and absorbed into the central stream, but it's not happening for some reason. I maybe altered myself too completely. Now I would rather live in the woods, would rather break into people's houses for a living than hang out with artists. I would rather rape my own mother than write a dissertation.

Hey, bitch, I say. I'm standing over her. Wake up, bitch. Wake up, bitch. I can't keep the image of her up. It goes flaccid then vanishes. She's too far away. I wander through the beautiful house alone.

MOVIES

I hyperfocus on hobbies to the exclusion of everything else. When I was in eleventh grade, recovering from nervous collapse and didn't want to use the internet, I fixated on watching movies.

One I watched many times during this period is called *Angst*. It is Austrian, made in the year 1983. The director, Gerald Kargl, went into debt to make the film, ruining his career. There are two versions of the film. The director prefers a shorter version. I prefer a longer version. I recommend finding both versions and watching the shorter version first—ideally in the middle of the night, when the world outside your home seems literally dead—then, immediately upon the conclusion of the film, watching the longer version.

The film is about the real-life exploits of Werner Kniesek. Werner Kniesek was born in 1946 in Salzburg, the fourth-largest city in Austria. When I think of Austria in 1946, I imagine a moonlike landscape, consisting primarily of white dust, plus occasional figures walking in and through the dust in a dazed and meaningless fashion. Allied bombing destroyed roughly half of the buildings of Salzburg. To the community Kniesek was born into, the end of the world had already occurred. Like many individuals who came into life during this period, Werner Kniesek never met his father.

In the film's opening moments, a camera bobs around an actor playing Kniesek, as though observing from the surface of a churning river. He approaches a random house and knocks on the door. When the resident—an older female—opens, Kniesek declares in German, "I am shooting now," and fires his gun into the woman. A montage of beautiful still images married to narration reveals that Kniesek was punished for this crime and spent several years in prison. This preamble is not present in the shorter version of the film, which begins when Kniesek gets out of prison. In any case, the film's feature-length central sequence (Kniesek exiting prison, wandering disoriented, performing a home invasion, and committing multiple murders therein) begins here.

I sometimes wonder what the odds are that someone will make a movie about my life. Don't laugh. When Werner Kniesek was in prison, contemplating his past crimes and planning his future ones, he probably felt like the most unpopular person in the world. The last thing on his mind was the possibility that someone would make a film about him. Such an idea would seem symptomatic of his psychosis. And yet, a talented filmmaker committed all his resources (and then some) to making a triumphant motion picture about this unremarkable man. Life is strange. For example, *The Amityville Horror* house was the site of a massacre in which a family was killed. Can you imagine being the guy who killed his family there, then watching Hollywood make dozens of movies about how nightmarish it is to hang out in the otherwise banal home where it happened? You, over there, doing nothing, consider the possibility that Hollywood will make a movie about your life. Consider also that it might be the most terrifying movie ever made. What might your role in such a film be, and what can you do, today, to ensure it will actually be made?

I confess I am fixated on the idea of home invasions. My two favorite novels are *The Stranger* by Albert Camus and *The Dwarf* by Pär Lagerkvist. But if I had to declare to you, the novels I believe are the most underrated, I would offer *Magnetic Field(s)* by Ron Loewinsohn, which is about home invasions, and *Limanora: The Island of Progress*, which is not. *Limanora: The Island of Progress*, written by Godfrey Sweven in 1903, is instead about a perfect society, or a number of perfect societies, something like the civilization that would develop if every house in the world was broken into, and every occupant brutally murdered, after which, mankind was replaced by something similar, but this time, actually interesting and good. I own a 1931 edition of *Limanora* in dust jacket and it's one of my most prized possessions. If our house was burning and I only had time to grab one item, I'd probably wander past my dad's aging housecat, Ralph, and find my copy of this book, then exit, Satan-like, as orange embers fall around me like the pedals and leaves of spectral flowers and trees.

While (somewhat) on the topic of Austrian films, another movie from that country I like is called *The Seventh Continent*. This film, like *Angst*, is based on an actual event, in this case a family who committed suicide together, but who, before doing so, flushed a large amount of money down the toilet. The central sequence in *The Seventh Continent* shows the family become something like a home invader *inside their own house*, destroying all of their possessions with a lack of affect and very flat feeling, in the way one can imagine dispensing with animals in a slaughterhouse, or killing civilians during a period of mass unrest, in a scenario where there is just nothing better, or more practical, to do with them.

This film contains acts of real violence, such as a fish tank being destroyed and real goldfish spilling onto the floor, and images of actors flushing actual money down a toilet. The filmmaker, Michael Haneke, accurately predicted that the most controversial aspect of the film would be the destruction of real currency, a taboo society finds intolerable. Within a theory-based rhetorical environment, violence, one can argue, is merely a social construct. It is whatever you want it to be. When a world becomes parodic, the destruction of money becomes violence.

The film's climactic sequence brings to mind *Home Alone*, one of the most popular films ever made, and, it should be said, a film centrally concerned with violent home invasion. But whereas in *Home Alone*, the occupant of the house is using items he finds in the house to protect the home from invaders—thereby siding with the house, and the idea of a family—in *The Seventh Continent*, the family rises up against the house, attacking the house itself, or apparent ghosts who occupy the house, or the idea of the house, or the idea of the family. They then punish themselves for this unthinkable affront to propriety and commit suicide, together, as one.

If I ever become a writer, I have thought that I maybe will write a sequel to my mother's essay, "A Theory of a Break-In," but from the fictive perspective of a cat burglar. In it, I would claim to be a man imprisoned for numerous home invasions and rapes. I would declare I read her essay while in prison, in attempting to *broaden my horizons*, and that, almost in spite of myself, found myself agreeing with her conclusions. I would also declare to the reader that I, the subject, have been reading a number of pieces of theory and believe I understand how this machine called theory works.

Theory, of the kind my mother wrote is ultimately a game, a parlor trick in which you conflate similes and metaphors for psychological insight in a way that is powerfully persuasive and emotionally suggestive, if not, ultimately, especially logical or accurate. The works of theory that a society elevates and makes widely available are those produced in its state-funded academies and academic presses—they represent explorations of topics powerful entities controlling society want us to look at, if only, in some cases, to distract us from topics they don't want us thinking about.

Despite the morally dubious nature of the enterprise of theory, interesting art can certainly be found in this realm. In fact, I really admire the work of Andrea Dworkin, whose paranoid rantings are rendered beautifully, and quite darkly. An interesting novel I bought in a used bookstore—I recognized it, as it used to be on my mom's bookshelf when I was growing up—is called *Airless Spaces*. It is feminist Shulamith Firestone's lightly fictionalized account of being imprisoned in a mental asylum. This work of fiction or memoir, or neither, fits, in my estimation, within an expanded definition of theory, if only barely.

Sitting in my jail cell (I'm once again a fictional character, narrating a response to "The Theory of a Break-In") I would *see* the author's examples of men being taught to break into conversations, or women's bodies, or spaces, as the author illustrates, and would *raise the stakes*, directing the reader to a 1973 film called *Forced Entry*, an early work of "hardcore" porn, concerned with a character, played by adult film star Harry Reems, who breaks into women's houses and rapes and murders them as a result of trauma experienced while serving in the Vietnam War. By naming the film *Forced Entry*, the filmmakers link the concept of home invasion to rape, and the fractal-like notion of invasions inside invasions. I would suggest that what goes on inside of the woman, as the sperm rushes through the forest of her body, surrounding the house, her ovum, and invading, that is itself a third invasion—revealing that our universe is a series of home invasions occurring inside other ones, infinitely, like a matryoshka doll, or a series of timed explosions, one after the other, in sequence, during the process of controlled demolition.

I conclude that we do not merely live in a rape culture; we live also in a home invasion culture, and that everything in our society, and in our lives, and all that we value and hold dear to is probably, in some certain light, akin to a burglar climbing in a window and destroying everything he finds.

FRIDAY, CONTINUED

I was watching *Angst* on the TV when she came down the steps. I was in her parents' house. She looked like a smeared Polaroid. Do you remember?

That was the night my relationship with her fell apart.

It was raining out and it smelled like electricity. The sky looked like purple velvet, ominous and creased.

We ran to the car to avoid the light falling rain.

"Where do you feel like going?" she said.

"I don't know," I said.

"Do you want to go to a party?"

"I thought we were going to see a movie," I said.

"I wish you had a phone so we could have talked about it."

She would always reference my not having a phone. We made plans ahead of time. I would say I'll pick you up on Friday at seven. It worked fine. I'll mention here that this was the sixth time I'd seen her. I guess we were in an in-between state, like between things becoming serious or falling apart. We had had sex two times, but it seemed odd to me, somehow off. She's the third girl I've been with in that way. The first girl was the one I dated between tenth and eleventh grade. Caroline. It sounds generic and embarrassing, but it was a summer relationship—is that a cliché? A summer romance when you're a teenager? There's something corny and embarrassing about that idea to me—it makes me think of a bad young adult novel for girls. In any case, it happened, then ended. I liked Caroline, but she called me crying one day and said that she was "in love" with another boy. What? She was hysterical. I thought it was slightly gross, but mostly just confusing and alienating. I don't have that kind of crazed emotional response to other people. She seemed like she had gone nuts. In retrospect, maybe she was more normal, and my response was odd. I think she was surprised I didn't freak out. I just stopped talking to her. Teenagers are supposed to lose their minds in front of their peers, it's like chicken pox, or something, you move through it then you're inoculated. I would like to think I felt something when we were together. I hold on to a little of the atmosphere of that time. Going to her pool a lot and hanging out at her mom's house. The chlorine smell of it. And the smell of her greasy dog. Even something about the air stirring a curtain, I must have watched something like that from her bed, because when I saw something like that in my room recently, it reminded me of Caroline—in any case, that episode was just a little blip in my life, and I think not very important. The other girl I met at a party. We went into a room. I could barely get an erection because the whole thing seemed so odd. I saw her another time and we didn't even look at each other, but it still technically counts I guess. Dill was the third. Each time we have gone up to her room, then I'm lying there, not sure what to do next.

"I guess I'll go now," I said.

"Well, do you want to hang out more," she said.

"No, I'm kind of tired," I said.

"It's only like 6 PM," she said.

Sometimes I feel like I run out of things to talk about. I have no idea what to say, and just want to be alone, without the potential for awkwardness, or errors, or drama.

On the Friday when she came down the steps, the Friday I watched some of *Angst* on her mother's TV, we hadn't had sex in two weeks. I wasn't sure I wanted to again. I think I found it disturbing and "pointless." I also felt like I was really bad at it and just felt weird doing it, like something larval under a heat lamp, naked and squirming. I just didn't like it.

"We can go to a party," I said. "But what does it have to do with me having a phone?"

"It's just my mom doesn't believe you don't have a phone. It is kind of weird. So she thinks you're lying about not having a phone."

"Why would I be lying about not having a phone?"

"I guess so they can't call you."

"Why would I avoid them calling me?"

"I don't know. It's what my mom said."

It was raining harder now and the whole thing felt off.

We went to a house with a bunch of cars parked in front and dumb-looking kids smoking cigarettes on the porch. I parked and just sat there.

"What," she said.

"What do you mean?" I said.

"You're acting weird," she said.

"How am I acting weird?"

"You're just acting weird, and I feel like you don't like me."

"I like you."

"Well let's go in then."

"I just want to sit here a minute. I have anxiety," I said.

"I have anxiety too," she said.

I closed my eyes a while. When I opened them everyone was inside.

"Are you ready to go in," she said.

"I guess," I said.

The front door was unlocked. The bright interior revealed fifty thousand dollars' worth of ugly McMansion decor. Everything brown or gray. Wall art told the family what to do. *Gather . . . Eat . . . Relax.* No one was around. Everything seemed to be happening on a deck where muffled sound came from.

Dill walked that way and I just followed. I entertained rosy dreams of vanishing like Batman, and never fucking again, quitting society tonight. But I was already here; why not take a few more steps into the night?

On the deck it was a couple alty kids and then a larger group of these wigger and mulatto guys in the corner, like holding up phones and yelling and doing fake gang signs and sticking out their tongues. The deck was bright but everything beyond them was dark hills and purple sky and rain.

"Hey," one of those kids said.

It was a somewhat fat half-black kid in a Supreme shirt.

"Hey," he said, "Bro! Hey, bro."

He was looking at me.

"I like your shirt," he said.

"Yeah, bro look at bro's shirt."

"Wow, that shirt is amazing."

"My shirt is amazing?" I said.

"My shirt is amazing?" one of the mulatto kids imitated, then grinned.

"Yeah, bro, look at your shirt bro. That shirt is fire."

I was wearing a faded Pantera shirt I got from work. Behind the boys, the black hills of remote suburbs—big well-kept lawns separated overlarge houses, spaced irregularly, like chunks of stone after a bombing. Mute lightning slashed the horizon and a flashbulb effect revealed the arc of the land. After a delay, a dull mortar blast, like an underwater explosion.

People turned to look.

"Why do you like my shirt?" I yelled.

They turned back. "What?" someone said.

"Why do you like my shirt?" I yelled in a slightly crazy way.

"Why do you like my shirt?" a wigger boy imitated then laughed. Another punched his shoulder and said it again in a high-pitched voice, laughing. "Why do you like my shirt?"

"I'll give you two for your shirt, brah," a guy said to me. He pulled out a roll of money and held up two one-hundred-dollar bills. "Two?" he said, grinning, then bopped his head a little and looked around.

All the other kids started yelling, "Ohhhh! Wow!"

"You better take that, bruh. I think you need to take that cash, son. You look like you need that money," someone said.

The kid walked up to me. "That's fair, right?"

"OK, sure," I said.

I went to use the bathroom. There were two blurry figures inside, doing drugs or something. They seemed scared of me.

"Sorry," I said, closing the door.

When I got into the bathroom. I took my shirt off and zipped my coat up over my otherwise bare top half. Before leaving, I ripped the porcelain soap holder off the wall and gently placed it in the sink. My hand was bleeding a little. I held it up and looked in the mirror. I wiped the blood on a white towel, then paused to take in the scene. The tacky bathroom looked beautiful to me now.

We left after I got the money for the shirt. I knew not a ton about this, but black people and lower class whites started wearing vintage clothing because of stuff on Instagram and TikTok. I think he thought he ripped me off for the shirt, but it was from the 2000s and only worth about $60 on eBay or whatever, plus now it had blood on it. There's a certain kind of low-IQ sneaker collector—people into streetwear, sweatshop garbage like Nike, Off-White, Supreme, basically ghetto-brain people, who pay a lot for T-shirts from the '90s and see it as rare and valuable, like designer clothing, or a pair of ugly basketball shoes in the box. It was started by Travis Scott or something. The people all seem like they have lead poisoning.

"Those guys were really annoying," I said.

"They gave you two hundred dollars for your shirt. That seems good."

"I don't care about that. I just hate those trashy fucking kids."

"They're fine," she said, scrolling through her phone.

"No, they're not. They literally ruin civilization."

"What are you like a Nazi or something?"

"No, I actually want to see everything collapse."

"What, like the end of the world?"

"I unironically would like to see the end of the world," I said.

"You're fucked up," she said.

"This relationship is over," I said.

"OK," she said. After about two minutes she said, "It's really weird you don't have a phone."

I dropped her off and didn't say anything. On Monday I didn't go into work. I'm really sick of everything. Everyone else is on the other side of some fence. I am the only one here.

I miss something I can't even define.

OBJECT LESSON

When I was small, maybe nine or ten, I became imaginatively obsessed with a fictional family of bears I created in my mind. I called them The Bear Family. They lived in a dense and primeval forest environment, an expression of my desire to live in such an enchanted location. They slept in a cave by a rock wall. Sometimes they went wandering and would enter a bright clearing with view of a snowcapped mountain, foregrounded by luscious, almost heartbreakingly beautiful, streams and fields. There they gathered berries and fish, before retreating to the darkness of their forest home. I have never been to Switzerland, but the image to me seemed Swiss, if only an unreal and impossibly perfected variation on such a concept. Adding more details to their story, envisioning them doing various activities in this idealized, almost heavenlike environment was a screen saver–like "video" I watched in my mind when at school, or in a car, or on a subway, when I had a few minutes to kill, or felt repulsed by my immediate environment and needed an escape or balm.

Later, when I started thinking about life more deeply, and started posing moral questions to myself, I used this model family—the bears—to determine what choices in life are best, most sound. I thought about the ways animals shit, kneeling. I decided that the human body is meant to kneel when shitting and so I started perching on the toilet seat like a vulture guarding eggs. I thought about their diets, berries and raw meats, raw fish, and tried to get my diet closer to that, within reason. I thought also about the goals and ambitions of these idealized creatures, almost divine in my imagining, thriving in a state of radiant nature. I accept that my assumptions about what bears do, how they behave, their habits, etc. are probably not always accurate with respect to real-life bear behavior, but that wasn't the point. The point was the creation of an ideal, a perfected state, that I seemed intuitively to be aware of and could draw in my mind's eye, like a picture, a picture I could use as a compass, or polestar—and from which I could, and should, derive wisdom and guidance. Though there is a part of me—a fallen and sick, and extremely *human* part of me—that prefers ugliness, I will admit that beauty is rightness, and beauty is health, and beauty is truth. When I saw the bears behaving beautifully, I saw the bears behaving rightly. And when I had decisions to make, I tried to imagine the bears behaving that way—when this was impossible, or absurd, I decided that such a choice was unsound; when they performed an imagined act gracefully and intuitively, this was a path more so worth taking.

I tried to create a version of human life that is closest to this ideal, and made a number of changes to my life. But I realized that there were limits to the utility of this comparison as a tool, because what makes these bears appear natural and good is the degree to which they are not human. They are the antithesis of human civilization and convoluted human thinking, which is nothing more than being lost. They are beautiful because they are not human. Realizing this, I abandoned the model of the bears when analyzing the minor details of life, because the comparison is simply not applicable. The only thing the bears represent in their perfected nature is the insanity of all human behavior, and the depravity of all human ambition, and the wrongness of all that human beings represent.

HIKIKOMORI

I lost interest in movies roughly around the time eleventh grade ended. Before eleventh grade I was pretty social, but following my mental collapse and week in a psych ward, I cut off all my friendships, stopped hanging out with people. I really just wanted to be alone. In retreating more completely from society, I devoted myself to hobbies. Once movies started to bore me, I found myself in a kind of crisis, with nothing even to catch in the trap of my mind, to turn over and consider in the ambient hologram of scholarship that makes life tolerable for me.

Walking to the bus stop after school, guys in white coveralls were taking trash out of a house and leaving it by the road. I noticed a little strange looking TV, shaped like one of those metal cages you trap squirrels in. It's called a Sony Trinitron, model SSM 14N5U, and was used in industrial and medical settings in the late twentieth century. I bought a Sony PlayStation and Sega Saturn at a vintage game store to use with it, but I didn't really know anything about video games. I was looking for games with strange atmospheres to go with this odd TV I found.

"Are there any games where someone just walks around?"

"I don't think we have anything like that," the clerk said.

I found ways to run burned discs on the systems and became somewhat addicted to video games, particularly Japanese role-playing games. This hobby got me through twelfth grade. I started to become interested in Japanese nerd culture. I watched anime. This began as a somewhat self-aware, ironic interest, an affectation I found stylish—I normally gravitated to highbrow stuff—but then it began to feel more genuine, even comforting. I even started researching Japanese murderers, Tsutomu Miyazaki, Issei Sagawa, and Tomohiro Katō, whom I found more interesting than Western killers, and read Japanese novels I liked by Osamu Dazai, Kōbō Abe, and Ryu Murakami.

When I graduated high school, and wasn't going to be attending college, I decided to become a self-aware otaku—this is a word for someone who has all-consuming interests—and even the more extreme form of otaku, hikikomori—a man who turns away from society in favor of his interests, or in some cases, pure solitude. I started thinking deeply about hikikomori, believing them to be the inheritors of an older Japanese tradition, rejecting the mongrelized Japanese society that merged with American "values" after WWII. They pursue beauty by turning their lives into a peaceful protest of life under capitalism by truly breaking away. This is the antithesis of the pseudo-politics of activists who, in their speech, reject the regime and its strictures, but who in their actions submit their body to the gauntlet of school, and work, and family—and really, it must be said, want little more than a pat on the head by their masters; even their fake rebellion seems oriented toward this goal. Hikikomori say no. They say I will let my burden fall so to become that most loathed thing, the useless man.

There is even an anime about the life of a hikikomori, called *Welcome to the N.H.K.* In its more serious moments, it captures something of the languor of that lifestyle. The character whittles away hours in a state of sublime privacy, doing little more than watching colors change in the window in his apartment. There is something beautiful about being alone in a small room, almost lost in the room, as the hours recede invisibly, like candle wax, or the burning away of dew by the morning sun. The summer morning feeling of stillness, as one focuses on almost imperceptible phenomena, like the movements of clouds as observed from a bed; the path of an insect wandering over floorboards; the emergence and disappearance of shadows; the percussive feet of rain, like the migration of gnomes; or the opening and closing of radiant gills, rendered on a wall, as late day sun pours through light-lacquered blinds.

These observations were those I viewed as "Japanese," and therefore hikikomori.

There is nothing beautiful in the constant movement of the active lifestyle, which seems in fact to exist to shut out the possibility of beauty, which, to apprehend, requires stillness and sensitivity and repose. The ideology of activity and "productivity" is anti-beauty; it is an ideology of power and illusion, of work and of movement; it bolsters the complex projection human society exists under and inside of, like a biodome. The absurd abstractions that motivate man—affirmed by activity and "productivity"—are revealed to be false, mere vapor, when viewed by any nonhuman perspective. Delusions like markets, business, money, and growth are not benign phantoms; they are more like destructive demons as they turn the surface of the world into a burned husk, something spent, long ago converted into "market value."

To be absorbed in this ideology of human confusion is to become blind to the reality of the world. There is no productivity, except maybe, in the development of specific feelings; in *that* there is the possibility of productivity, the production of peace, or calm, or a feeling of beauty, and the connection to a moment, as it is being lived, the only external thing one possibly, with great focus, can hold in his hand. Everything else is an idea or an object, easy to form opinions of, but always external and alien. Objects are things one can see, and consider, but cannot truly know or possess. A moment one fixes his sights on, perceiving it as it passes, this is the one external thing a person, maybe, can grab, and merge with. By becoming hikikomori and studying Japanese society, I would get closer to the fragile flame of truth and would learn to hold a moment in my hand in a state of perfected stillness.

I wanted to turn my bedroom into a perfected hikikomori space, everything in primary colors, like a parody of a '90s playroom, like an abandoned or uncanny version of FAO Schwarz, and where I, the centerpiece, would lay, deteriorating, in bed—ideally upon an absurd pencil-themed bed frame like I once saw in a family comedy from the mid-nineties, and maybe surrounded by bold outer space–themed wallpaper, or perhaps a monochromatic grid, interrupted by colorful geometric shapes, like the cover of an old algebra textbook, but spray-painted and torn and dirty, everything together representing an inspired parody of my status as a useless adult child and the world's eternal son, playing video games and watching cartoons in an environment of sublime disorder and radical, aestheticized refusal until my body gives up the ghost, and I transmogrify into something new, something better.

I was several hours into *Final Fantasy VII* when my mom died. Like an event in a video game, this plot twist sent me on a different path. On that day, I kicked my TV off the desk. I tried to make it work again but it was broken. I boxed up everything associated with my hikikomori phase and left the TV out with the trash, just like how I found it several years earlier.

JOB UNTITLED

After the bad night with Dill, I mostly just stayed in bed.

"Are you not going to that job anymore?" my dad asked after a few days.

"I'm not sure," I said.

"It seems like a shitty job," my dad said.

"What is a good job?" I asked him. I genuinely couldn't differentiate a good job from a bad job. Some jobs paid more than other jobs, but otherwise they all seemed the same.

"Someplace where the people respect you."

"Why does it matter if the people respect you?"

He squinted at me. He was wearing a robe and holding a cup of coffee. He seemed too tired to have this conversation and just walked out of the room.

JOB REDUX

On a Monday two weeks after I stopped going in, I decided to see if I still had a job at the clothing recycler.

I walked in (a little nervous) and found the manager guy Marco, who seemed to oversee everything.

"I got Covid," I said, grabbing my throat and miming a cough.

"Oh, you get Covie?" he said with polite mock alarm.

"Yeah I get Covie. But I call. Telephono," I said, lying.

The phone in the office with the bird rang all day. No one ever picked it up.

"OK, OK, you worky?"

He pointed to the area of the warehouse where I used to sort clothes. There was a Hispanic woman with a space heater now.

"Still sick," I said, grabbing my throat. "Still Covie."

"OK, OK. You no feel sick and you can worky, OK."

"OK," I said.

"A girl looky for you."

"A girl?"

"Your sister. She looky for you."

He held up a finger then walked away.

My sister . . .

When he came back, he gave me a folded-up note with my name on it.

> *I'm sorry for how I was the last time we hung out. I could tell you didn't like me asking you about your phone. One time you said why do you always talk about me getting a phone. You don't want a phone and I wasn't respectful of that. You are different than other people. I would like to spend more time with you. I hope we can do something soon.*
>
> *Dill*

In August, I decided to start trying. It brought me to where I am now. I need to keep trying, keep seeing if there is something for me here.

This is the end of one stage of my life, but the beginning of another.

YOUTUBE

I started my YouTube channel when I was thirteen. I reacted to dashcam videos, public freakouts, bodycam footage. It was like satirical, but nihilist-absurdist? My account was called doombuggy, then glyphosate. My most popular series was called "the round-up"—I would livestream a series of videos I had previously edited and sewn together, like, someone fighting police, or acting dumb at a protest, or throwing things in a Burger King, whatever was entertaining, and spontaneously add sound effects, air horns, primitive graphics, like an elephant stampede, or whatever. In the corner of the videos, there I was, reacting. (My dad made the horrifying observation that what I was doing was somehow akin to being a DJ. He thought I would like that, but I can't think of anything more embarrassing and repulsive than being a DJ.) I wanted the streams to seem truly chaotic, like something that might cause brain damage or permanently darken someone's outlook. Bouncing in my chair with chunky headphones on, I replicated the behavior of other streamers, who I was kind of making fun of but also imitating? Taking what they did that was working, then making fun of the rest. Also pretending I was nuts and laughing insanely, but in a fake, ironic way. Something like that . . .

I started posting on Twitter under the name glyph0sate. I was in a group chat with a bunch of funny and nihilistic "Nazi" people. We would just share videos we found and I don't think anyone was very serious. One guy said he got visited by the FBI after he pictured himself with his uncle's AR-15. In retrospect, I don't really know anything about the people I was talking to, even though it all seemed very ironic and jokey, maybe some had dark designs. Everyone in the chat knew about my YouTube channel where you could see my face. It probably would have been really easy to link my face to rude comments I made and get me in trouble in a way that would follow me my whole life. I think in a certain way I wanted that. I think I thought that seemed good. I wanted there to be consequences for my speech, consequences for being myself in America. It seemed absurd but also perfect. External consequences never came, but the waiting for them, combined with something about spending so much time online—this feeling of high agitation, high stimulation, but while sitting still in a darkened room, watching videos of cars crashing, people bleeding, animals dying—at the end of it, you are changed.

The channel became more and more popular. The feeling of popularity made me feel like I was losing control. Too many people were looking at me. I was too much an idea in other people's minds. In popularity there's an aspect of pollinating the world with an idea of yourself that you're either able to deal with or that makes you uncomfortable. It's a two-way mirror. The illusion of aloneness, but people are observing, scrutinizing. The watched person seems dominant, but it's the other way around. In a video game, they have cover; you're exposed. They plan out attacks. I don't know they're there. They count my pores. I see murk.

Someone made a thread about my channel on 4chan. Some people said I was retarded. Other people liked my channel. Another wondered is he "/our guy/"—this meant is he a racist, a Trumpist, that sort of thing. I started talking to a guy who made similar videos. In truth, his videos were a rip-off of mine. I actually had a little fanbase during this period—they would hang out in my chat, donate 5 dollars sometimes. I claimed I had just graduated high school; in reality I was fourteen, maybe fifteen. "Do you think the world is going to end?" he asked me. "Yeah, probably," I said. It didn't really matter either way. Looking for content to add to my video collages I would stay up all night watching boring, but also numbing videos of people being arrested or surveilled, exploring abandoned houses and malls, killing themselves, fighting, falling down, bleeding.

I was worried I was going to get strikes for reusing footage I found—even though I heavily manipulated all of it, putting watery filters over everything, saturating or desaturating colors, stretching, zooming, slowing down, speeding up—inadvertently developing an aesthetic of funhouse nightmare. That my videos felt political—but weren't really; they were merely violent and chaotic—made me feel I was going to get banned, which scared me. I spent so much time online, the idea of getting banned was akin to coming home and finding all the locks on my house had changed. Alternatively I thought I was going to get doxxed, ruin my irl existence in a way I couldn't currently calculate, but that would drive me insane in the years to come, shorten my life, disgrace my family, maybe cause bricks to get thrown at my dad's house or wake up to find his car was spray-painted, or maybe just be swept up in some internet dragnet or something, get added to lists I could never access but that invisibly circumscribed all options for me moving forward. But I hadn't even done anything? I really just wanted to be creative and have a place to be—it sounds corny but I really just wanted to belong somewhere. From so far outside of it, I struggle to explain the tense and uneasy cloud I was wandering into. In retrospect, I realize I was becoming literally psychotic.

*

Tenth grade ended; that summer, I think I spent at least fourteen hours a day on the computer. My dad left me alone. He could see my videos were becoming popular and I was good at editing, good at using the computer. I hated school and got horrible grades, barely making it from one grade to the next. What I was developing seemed practical actually, weirdly. I used my dad's credit card to order drugs I read about online—I ordered modafinil from India, which was supposed to keep me up for days, but didn't really do anything. I ordered kratom from Thailand, which gave me a lightly opiated, dreamy feeling but mostly made me want to puke, and large amounts of dextromethorphan from Amazon—generic Robitussin, basically but in a formulation designed expressly for drug abuse and hallucination. I didn't really want to get high. I think I just wanted to sit in the seat longer, find a way to get more performance out of my brain. Everything blurred. The drugs fixed my anxiety, except when it came whooshing back, carrying me away and inaugurating phases where I stayed up all night muttering to myself, chattering out little bleep-blurp sounds that had no meaning. I felt good, most of the time, but without realizing it, I had lost all contact with a shared conception of the world. I was seeing things that other people were not seeing, making novel connections, but I was lost—in the midst of that lostness, there were moments of absolute beauty. Like when in the middle of the night I walked into the woods, saw shapes there. Or when I viewed a blurry video about the murder of Jesus Christ and wept, deciding it was all real.

Was I going to be crucified also?

It certainly seemed possible.

KILLING MY SON

Are you familiar with the term homunculus? Near the end of the summer before eleventh grade, I actually made one. I don't need you to believe me. I will simply tell you about it. It was supposed to be funny. It wasn't funny at all.

As part of a series called "glyphosate tries" I made parodies of other videos popular at the time, such as the time I pretended to break into an abandoned house only to be confronted by a big bucket of talking slime in the basement. The slime, within the mythos of the video, had led many earlier lives, such as a Waffen SS field commander who died on the Eastern Front, then a West German prostitute who died of loneliness in 1987. I listened to its tale, then dumped it out in the backyard, releasing its constrained soul and allowing its essence to dissipate peacefully. Another time, I sampled a new fast-food sandwich, but instead of eating the food, I just ordered it and sat in the parking lot, improvising an eerie monologue about child actors who died of drug overdoses, never even opening the bag.

A YouTuber from Russia captured my attention. In his tutorial-like videos, he claimed to make a living homunculus by injecting chicken eggs with human semen, incubating the egg under a heat lamp, then extracting a black wormy creature that writhed around on a table or lived a few hours in a chemical solution.

I was intrigued, even somewhat stirred by the clinical tone of the videos and details such as blurred images of human semen and the narrator speaking through a gas mask, afraid of his own creation—to say nothing of the actual animal, a writhing sluglike creature that, even if fake, was extremely convincing. Researching what I thought was a made-up internet term like jenkem or slenderman, I discovered a rich history related to the mystical homunculus. An early reference to this creature is to be found in the *Book of the Cow*, an ancient Arabic manuscript. The "recipe" therein calls for the mixing of human semen and animal blood, which is to be injected into the female sex of a cow or ewe. The inseminated animal is smeared in the blood of a sacrificed beast and forced to consume its meat. A mixed solution is released from the creature's sex. The mother is killed at that stage and the fledgling homunculus left to bathe in its blood, whose energies are mixed. Eventually a spot of hardness emerges, then a tiny evil man. Other formulations appear in a variety of mystic texts, some simple, some complicated. They emerged from a wide variety of antique civilizations in documents carefully protected and passed down; those strange creatures of lore, separated by languages, cultures, oceans, and centuries, were mysteriously linked, sometimes sharing uncanny similarities . . .

REDPILL

What do you believe in? I mean to say have your expectations ever been completely violated by experiences you had or discoveries you made? Material that fits under the rubric of "conspiracy" provides that experience for people in the modern world. There is a feeling of shock and loss in the sensation of being "redpilled." This utterly modern form of alienation can be as thrilling as a ride on a roller coaster or a drug binge. When formerly normal people snap and attack public places with body armor and assault rifles, they are writing the final chapter of their redpill experience; invariably, they are people whose lives were changed by alarming discoveries, a feeling of the world becoming unreal, with all the attendant violation and horror such an idea implies. They were changed, and wanted to change the world, or at the very least, pass it a note in class, leave it a few last lines on a chalkboard, even if the meaning of those thoughts is blurry and confounding. The action itself is the clearest statement. Without ambiguity, they have declared that it is more appropriate to produce a shock wave than slip away silently, like someone ashamed. Instead of letting the ball hit you in the head, volley it back, they seem to say, because by the time it gets to your opponent, it may have transformed into a tsunami large enough to erase the world.

As you probably know, the process of being "redpilled" is a metaphor derived from *The Matrix*. It sees a person realize he occupies a world of illusions, a carefully constructed fake reality, more like a computer's graphical interface than anything we can truly call a nest or home. This fake reality is loaded with incentives, embedded like easter eggs in the environment: women to seduce, objects to buy, dazzling one-time experiences to slip into and be changed by—make sure you take a picture so you can remind yourself this is something you did. Isn't human society amazing? In reality the individual is merely falling through life, a chrome marble in a pinball machine, low-intensity current zapping a few secondhand thoughts and behaviors into inevitability. Their inner life is a dismal blend of mimicry and inheritance; a primitive gadget hammering out Morse code–like messages from circumscribed options. His family is pastiche made flesh, objectively superfluous. Look into their hearts: they are less so spiritual beings than something like a wind turbine or solar panel or automobile battery, a tiny reserve of economic value, plus a slapped-on sticker or logo—USDA Grade A. They lament how hard they work, how much they suffer. All they have earned is their own annihilation, their absolute erasure. "Average" people should have their blood drained for the Red Cross. Then the limp bag of guts and bones should be thrown into a threshing machine. That's what they think is normal when it comes to animals. Of course, the only creature that deserves that kind of treatment is them.

Life for me has been little more than a series of shocking revelations, revealing only the horror and stupidity of the world. When I went to a psychiatrist, my father sat in with us for the first session. He spoke briefly, revealing his true thoughts about how he sees me. My father described me as alienated. I do not believe I am alienated. I believe it is amazing that I am as integrated into the world as I am. He said I am intelligent but don't apply myself. I truly was unable to do better at school than I did. It was impossible to pay attention to what the teachers were saying. When I took tests, tension blurred my thoughts. Sometimes I would try to study, but it was impossible to focus. Anger at these ridiculous exercises made it impossible to think straight, let alone "study." He said I don't care about anything. I care about a lot of things and am moved by art and beauty. I think constantly. I love words and ideas. I am just not the same species as them. It is impossible for others to understand me.

It's hard for me to think about this part, but I will try. I'm working through things, trying to sort through the past until I've processed my whole life. This really did happen: I set up a camera and masturbated into my hand. With a syringe, I injected a brown egg with my semen. I kept the egg warm. A little bug really was in there when I opened it up. It stunk so horribly. Something was really moving. It frightened me and I crushed it with my notebook. I really believe that's what happened. No, I wasn't a reliable person in those days, but it's what I experienced. It's what I feel I saw.

I concede the breakdown that came afterward can be read one of two ways.

DIGRESSIONS

In a dream I wrote a novel. In the novel I was a boy in a wheelchair in 1945 in Germany.

My house was bombed every day but I wheeled myself out on the patio to scream at the bombers.

I (the narrator of my novel) fell asleep in my wheelchair and in dreams saw blurred representations of the bombers in a variety of settings:

First, as insects, entering a tiny cave in the side of a brick, then, from the edge of a boat, twirling darkly at the bottom of the ocean, in the forms of mixed aquatic wildlife, primarily stingrays and sharks. Then in other settings, but that tore apart to dissolving whiteness as I woke up from my dream.

My neighbor was a twelve-year-old girl I was in love with and I smeared my bedsores with honey to keep them clean.

It wasn't a novel though.

I was the boy and I wrote a novel about America. I was the writer of a boy about Germany.

I was a wheelchair in the Black Forest in Germany. I had been tipped over and abandoned. I was gassed in the back of a truck, but I also did the gassing. I ate animals, but in death, I too was consumed.

Representing human tragedy, forest folk (whose heads were wide and pale, resembling hot dog buns) took pity on me and smeared me with honey (I am a wheelchair again) which caused the tears in my leather to heal.

Gradually I developed. I had the strength to stand on my own four wheels, I mean my own two feet, and reentered society in order to serve mankind. I stand at the sink, shaving. Blood drips down.

I went to sleep at age twelve and woke up at age thirty-seven.

Some day soon I (a nineteen-year-old poet or pseudopoet) will be freed from all numbers, memories, and representations. I'm just kidding, haha. I'll go take a nap now. Thank you for reading this.

I wrote the above "poem" in a notebook and handed it to my father. I assembled it from several drafts, and believe it or not, this brief and pathetic work was the product of several hours of mental labor, trying to find, and then cleanly render images that seemed intriguing to me. The final paragraph I added just before finishing, with a feeling of some panic—embarrassed—hoping to thin what seemed like pure weirdness and self-seriousness. Hedging.

"Don't quit your day job," he said, laughing.

I laughed along, embarrassed. When he left the room, I reread the paper. OK, sure, this isn't exactly right—but he, a professional writer, can't even see what I'm trying to do? The feelings I'm trying to convey? The final paragraph spared me. It would seem a cry for help otherwise.

I threw the paper away. I'm a fool. My writing career has ended four hours in.

*

There was a man who broke into a house, trying to subsist. He was on drugs. In jail he read his two favorite novels back-to-back, *The Stranger* by Albert Camus and then the *The Dwarf* by Pär Lagerkvist. He had brain lesions due to drug use and his sedentary lifestyle which worsened his anhedonia, and now caused his life to become a psychedelic hell; white worms slid along the inside of his eyelids.

Those two books, both composed during the final years of the Third Reich, while in its cradle, contained some linked character he became obsessed with, deciding in his delirium it a single work that God authored and provided him. Meursault became the dwarf while waiting to be freed as the modern world of *The Stranger* deteriorated into the pre-modern world of *The Dwarf*, perhaps after the catastrophe of some unreal war. Meursault became more exuberant but also unhinged.

This was a story I wrote in bed, while trying to sleep, but I don't have paper. I don't need it. The story is about me at age forty. Something like the life I'm wandering into.

I gave this story to my dad by way of living it over the course of many years. It was my day job.

He wasn't laughing any more.

My mental health has been a disaster since age sixteen.

TEENAGE BREAKDOWN

"He is having a breakdown," my father said. "It's an emergency. He broke the TV."

My father came home and I was screaming.

"I killed my son. I killed my son," I was apparently yelling.

I had started eleventh grade just one day earlier. I wasn't ready to go back to school. I was really out of it. I had been staying up all night. I had a terror of going back to school. I didn't know what school was. On the night before the first day of eleventh grade, I didn't sleep at all. I barely slept the night before that. All day people looked at me weird and said, Are you OK? in slow motion. I have no idea what I said in response. I walked into the wrong classroom. The teacher said to go away. I stood there. I didn't understand what he was saying. He thought I was stoned. He thought I smoked weed and went to school. I said, I'm not that kind of kid. I remember he looked confused and said, this is not your class, and pointed to the print-out of my schedule crumpled in my hand. I really didn't understand what he was saying. Aren't I supposed to be here? I said. I thought he was singling me out for some kind of discipline. Kids in the class were laughing. Some were quiet and seemed afraid, of me, for me, I'm still not sure. He realized I really wasn't able to understand language and his look changed from anger to alarm. He grabbed my arm and escorted me to the nurse. I didn't sleep last night, I told her. They called my dad and he picked me up. You need to take better care of your health, my dad said. No more staying up on the computer all night. I wasn't on the computer. I was awake in bed, rolling around, like they tell you to do if you're on fire. I didn't sleep that night either. Something was wrong with my brain. Things got worse and worse.

*

Just before this period, in the weeks and months preceding the breakdown, I got really into watching the wrong kind of thing, doing the wrong kind of research. I think they call this a "pipeline." It started with gore. There was the suicide of Bjork's stalker. That was one of the first videos that made a big impression. His name was Ricardo Lopez. In the 1990s, he videotaped himself, and shot himself in the head. He painted his face red and black, like Darth Maul. He was involved with unusual mailings.

Then there was the 1987 R. Budd Dwyer video. A politician made chaotic statements at a dais, handed out envelopes, then pulled out a Dirty Harry–style revolver and shot himself. I studied his nose, that it became a soda fountain of blood, and realized at that moment that we are pressurized bags, tunnels of flesh, and that our blood is always looking for a way out but is instead kept inside and looped around, cycled, like a figure eight—and it was a moment when I considered darkly the incredible complexity of our bodies, the engineering of it all, allegedly random, the accretion of randomness over a long time horizon; which, was a theory, though less accurate seeming than the more obvious one—that some subterranean intelligence, some kind of invisible will—electromagnetism—organized our shape in collaboration with God? Something like the T-1000 in *Terminator 2* forming from splattered droplets—but in atoms. Did you know that atoms are 99 percent air, we are electrical sculptures is all, kept together by an electrical frequency—this frequency is God. Humming is tuning in. I could have turned hippie, but instead became darkwave Christian. Wait. This is being a Christian? I decided yes, and during this time used vast torrents of mental energy to marry anti-Darwin ponderings to the beautiful poetry of The King James Bible, plus hate videos I was finding online. My new philosophy had parallels in the way I now saw nature: something sewn together into truth from the force of magic vision.

    I got caught up with conspiracy. JFK. The Zapruder tape. The president became a Venus flytrap. His wife reached back passionately, like the figure on the cover a Harlequin novel from the '70s. Around this time, a curse was placed on me that made it hard to sleep, but, in exchange, revealed the demon layer hidden, like wiring, behind the walls of the world. One night, I saw those black smoky figures. I would describe them as socklike. Then the light came in, and my dad was standing in the doorway, his face disfigured, like a Looney Tunes Picasso. On to September 11. I watched blurry documentaries, listened to phone calls from passengers. Some of them whispered little secrets onto the answering machine. "It's a frame," one victim said. Was anyone even on the planes? Were they planes at all? One critic said they were missiles in airplane drag, Styrofoam wings for good measure. The whole thing was a projection of some kind. There was molten metal dripping brightly at the base of the disaster, like some kind of hellish spring. This had some meaning.

Thermite. Termite. I was putting it all together. I saw images of the towers in motion, then frozen, irregularities circled, like a football broadcast. The dust became like spray foam, tumbling over itself upon the roadways of New York City; the city became cavities in a wall in an abandoned house Mexicans were outfitting with insulation. I was taken with the beauty of these theories. The towers didn't merely crumble; they seemed thumbed down into the earth by Baal. Suggestions of a demonic event. A UFO in the skies just before the collapse, visible in several tapes. Then the dazed people in frocks of gray dust, like Pompeii victims reanimated by sorcerers. At the center of my concerns was Israel. There were clues in the names of things. To kiss the Wailing Wall meant sacrificed babies and animals would weep in perpetuity. If I was concerned that none of it was real, the name of the country said think again—It Is Real.

*

"Upload something," one guy said in a group chat. I stopped streaming around this time, feeling I was in a transitional phase: too awake for streaming, too nascent to explain the phenomenon swimming around me.

"I believe that frogs will soon be falling from the sky," I said. This had something to do with Pepe the Frog, but also the character from *Chrono Trigger* who carried a sword, also Baal—and some vague thoughts I was having about the end of the world.

"What do you mean?" one guy said.

"My channel is on hiatus," I declared.

I exited group chat on Twitter then deleted my account.

I was on my own now, and taking the first steps that, in time, would make me anti-computer. But before that, I had to go completely insane.

*

I got into bed after the first day of school, a failed attempt at being human. I hadn't slept in days. I remember hoping I would sleep that night. I remember at around seven, as the sun began to go down, I started thinking about a video I had watched several months earlier called *The Real Israel* by Reverend Ted Pike. In a series of videos made in the late '80s and early '90s, Ted Pike pulled back the curtain on the perfidious Jews, vampiric devil-worshippers—truly the synagogue of Satan. The blood of Christians was akin to gasoline in fueling Kabbalistic attacks. Consider when the world turned. The world of two thousand years ago made some sense, seemed livable, coherent. The primitive world, wild and free, with these tiny and extremely varied little incarnations of man—something like the differing colors and abilities of Yoshi in *Super Mario World*—distributed like Easter eggs onto the many and variously varied landscapes of the world. I saw them from above, like I was in an airplane, or was an airplane, anthropomorphic, with a gray-blue polished face, like a spraypaint huffer. My movements drew arrows over the face of the world, evoking *Triumph of the Will* and *Street Fighter II*. Cartoon savages waved at me from the continent of Africa, Man in beige safari dress waved from Australia. In Europe, Bavarian types in lederhosen pushed eastward, then were pushed back, wandered dazed through rubble, found dingy swastikas in the dirt. I went back in time, like a video of smoke sucked back into a bottle. Great wooden ships hovered over the oceans, giving the world the look of a real-time strategy game. Mayans beside their pyramids in South America sacrificed babies, and I reversed, was dragged over Europe backward, saw Black Plague and Bronze Age, then settled over the Middle East as hunched Jews oversaw the nailing of Christ to the cross but massively, like a vast hologram and I watched everyone crying and screaming. Then I saw the movements of these murderous Jews over the centuries. Because, you see, when Jesus Christ was killed, a curse was placed on the Jews who rejected him. Those cursed Jews traveled around the world. They weren't themselves bad, but they had something like a cursed shadow that ruined the nations they entered. It was a corrupting energy. The Rothschilds—my children, the patriarch famously insisted, go to the centers of human activity, and their footprints turned the world bad; by the time they had seen everything, turned the whole world bad, or parodic, they were to go back to Israel, and this dark Jesus, inverted Jesus, antichrist, would clear the world. And this made sense because—I was seeing the grand design—this is why the world exists—it is theater—the world is weird theater. The world is theater for God, his vivid aquarium; as I lay in bed that night, he was sharing the view with me, like a father and son on a ridge, nudging the boy and handing him binoculars. The sun came out in the morning. The blue undersea look, with the first bird sounds, then more—like water for coffee I'm heating in a pan—until it achieved the frantic boil of day, birds and bugs shrieking into light, panicked at being forced to live.

My dad came in. "Are you going to go to school today?"

"No," I said.

"If you're still like this tomorrow I think we should take you to a doctor," he said. "I'm worried about you."

"I'm fine," I said. I wanted to tell him about the Jews but didn't know where to start.

"I'm going to go to the store. Do you want anything?"

"Pedialyte and laxative, and a crucifix, if you can find one."

"I'm going to get you Pedialyte and a laxative," he said.

He left. Eventually I got up and looked at myself in the mirror.

I had two black eyes. Huh?

I got back into bed and started thinking about the homunculus. I decided I killed my son, and that killing my son had put a curse on me, like Jesus, like the Jews. I killed my son like my mom killed me—the world is just smaller and smaller representations of itself, infinitely—and the feeling of this got into me, like electricity, and I started screaming. I ran downstairs and broke the TV, threw some mugs, broke plates, screamed, pissed on the floor, the whole nine yards.

The police came and arrested me. I was taken somewhere. I barely remember.

In the mental hospital my mom came to visit. I saw her at the end of the hallway but went back into my room. She was wearing black. She didn't see me. Her hair was in a short style. I was still punishing her, for what, though? Her arrangement with my father. I felt guilt, but that's OK. One day I will fix things. Everything will work out in the end.

It wouldn't, though.

That was the last time I would see her.

After I got out of the mental hospital, I wasn't sure about much. I was on a variety of pills that made me tired all the time, but at least I was missing some school. I shuffled around the house like a patient and stared out the window. I became attached to calm and peace, activities like watching gills of light on a wall, or the rising of steam from coffee. These were healing feelings, that to me seemed "Japanese." I closed my eyes and wondered about the fate of my son, the homunculus. The rot inside the egg was alive. I picked up a notebook and jotted down the thoughts that channeled through me.

I am alone.

I am afraid.

I am with you.

Goodbye, son, I whispered.

I stuck the stained notebook beneath a pile of clothes and tried to forget every single thing about the internet.

DEAR MOM I

I had a dream the other night you were in. I was a kid and we went to Salem, Massachusetts for Halloween. The leaves bounced over the cobblestone like a stampede of wildebeest. Do they have cobblestone in Salem? We went there, for real one time, right? I ask because some memories of childhood are fake. For example, I dimly recall "Colonial Williamsburg." We ate whole chickens on pewter plates in a low-ceilinged and dark, "tavern-style" restaurant, then went down a spiral staircase into a fake dungeon, with dirt floors, and a rack, and one of those spiky sarcophaguses called an iron maiden. Dad says we never did that—I'm sure we did? That was maybe the first time I wanted to fix things with you, I wanted to ask you a question about something or the other, but it was too late; you're gone. That we weren't talking made it easier when you died, but it dragged out the distress, made the wound seem unclean. It prevented something like "closure," if that's even the right word. What is closure? It makes me think of stitches on Frankenstein's monster, or a suburban house with no front door, the wind always blurring in . . . Blurring in? Butting in. That's barely better. Sorry, I'm tired.

Things are the best they've ever been for me, well ever since age five, or so, and I'm thinking that everything may actually work out, an inconceivable idea as recently as a year ago. If you were still alive, we'd be working things out about now, but you're not, and we can't. I don't really feel bad about it. The way I reacted to this phrase—open marriage—was normal and fine, for someone like me who barely thinks about sex. A family has rules, and you and Dad both did things that broke the rules of love, that loosened these binds that were supposed to keep us together, sweetly. It was a curse, for sure, but I decided you're caught up with payments, and we'll try a jubilee. I used to think I was closer to Dad, but now I think I may be getting closer to you, for a number of reasons—one of which being that you're a ghost, and not even real. Another of which being that I actually read this book of yours, the idea of which drove me quite literally insane, called *Sex Lives* and actually liked it, though it was probably only tolerable because you're dead; the sex lives of the dead are merely tragic, rather than passionate and "hot."

I have wondered if you would have tried to squeeze me through some kind of "trans" remaking had our family stayed together. You loved that kind of "woke" messaging in life. I don't think I would have agreed to it. But if I had been chemically castrated, medically edited, I think it could have turned me into a better artist, made me feel more inhuman. I imagine me with a shaved head and pathetic little breasts and a tiny penis and a chain around my neck. Would someone just nail zim to a cross already? Why am I besotted with images of crucifixion? The opposite of the self-aggrandizing politics of normal people. The idea of a wormlike freak, a capital T on the horizon and covered in blood, the most expensive Halloween decoration at Home Depot. His agony so titanic it releases a spiritual emission worthy of documentation, if not a white-robed cult. Is that the nature of a curse? A crime so rancid it causes a stain? I once thought I cursed myself by committing a murder, but now think I merely crushed a rotten yolk while high on dissociatives. In truth, I'm not sure what happened, but I'm sticking with that earthbound theory to keep life (minimally) tolerable.

I haven't been taking my medication, because I've wanted to live life more consciously, if dangerously. I had this weird vision I wanted to ask you about. I believe my name is not Armand, but Armilus, and that you are not a woman, but a stone? This isn't a "dead fish" joke; I mean to say are you made of stone? Maybe a metaphor, regarding your coldness and distance. If they have Google in heaven, type in "Armilus" and tell me what you think. I sometimes believe the end of the world is coming, and I alone got the tip-off. Would it be possible for you to visit me and reassure me that everything will be OK? Soften your heart of stone and try now to reach me, You rarely did this in life, so it seems just as likely you might do it in death. The sun is coming up now. Congratulations, Mom, my dead mother's become my imaginary friend. One last thing. What does this mean:

"*the worms never die and the fire never outs*"

I saw that phrase in a dream—does it mean I'm already in hell? Or that the age of prophecy and prediction is over, and that God really is dead, disseminated into, at best, brainless static electricity? Please tell me that this notion isn't true, and we're not all trapped in an "economy" rather than a mystic text?

Talk soon,
Armie

*

"Who are you talking to?" Dill asked.

I was sitting alone in our new apartment. Looking out the window.

"Nobody."

THE EXTREMIST

Did you hear about the bookstore shooting a year ago? A man walked into a bookstore in Moline, Illinois, let off some fireworks, and shot a 9mm handgun into the haze. Two people died, including my mother, Judith Meyer, and a retired public school teacher, Jacqueline Weir. Several additional women were variously injured.

The attack was a national news item for a week and a half. Interesting or notable details about the crime included the setting, a feminist bookstore called Turning Pages, and the death of a nationally known writer. The murderer's forum comments and a YouTube channel was described as a troubling trail. Twenty-five years earlier he had appeared as a teenage vampire on several daytime talk shows.

Notable, for a few hours in the period immediately following the crime, was the killer's not having been apprehended at the site, but rather fleeing the scene. He was confronted at his residence the following morning. These details stretched the drama and introduced the thrill of the "manhunt," then the "standoff."

The killer, John Merso, was albino, nominally half-black, with a pink complexion. He had a pygmy mouse look and usually wore a hat. He lived in twelve different states. He was involved with goth and vampire subcultures in the 1990s but veered from that in recent years. The albinism detail seemed a complicating turnoff to media, who avoided leading with his tragic and jarring portrait, preferring instead an image recovered from a gas station. This full-body representation, ominous and vague, oriented on a dark blur in the frame's lower right corner.

John Merso's life can be reasonably described as an American odyssey. At or near the end of this odyssey he returned home to the Midwest. ("The Prodigal Son," was the name of one of the videos on his YouTube channel.) In Moline he stayed with his ailing mother. During this time he worked at a supermarket. He was attempting to build a house with a family member, a sometimes builder, but this final hopeful project stalled, beginning at or near this time, his life's violent final phase.

He killed his mother three days before the attack. Death count: one. He finished preparing for and executed his attack on the bookstore. Death count: three. Police found him at his home, his mother's home, and killed him. In total, four individuals died.

John Merso, 48
Rebecca Merso, 76
Judith Meyer, 44
Jacqueline Weir, 67

Attacks of this kind develop "legs"—Columbine, Pulse Nightclub, Christchurch, San Bernardino—and graduate to the status of signal events, symbolic of epochs and movements, or don't, instead migrating to the invisible graveyard of forgotten crime. In George Orwell's novel *Nineteen Eighty-Four*, news items intentionally erased from public consciousness are sent down the "memory hole." In America, there is something like a memory hole, though it is less a government tool than the incidental final resting place of news items that for ambiguous reasons fail to create lasting impact and recognition.

One year later, the 2023 Turning Pages bookstore shooting is halfway down the American memory hole.

*

In the 1990s, John Merso dressed in gothic clothing and sometimes wore red contact lenses and fake vampire teeth. "Are you a musician?" the host of a talk show asked him. "No, I'm just John," he replied, then hissed, unveiling fangs.

"But John is a vampire. Isn't that right?" the host said.

"I identify as a vampire, I identify as bisexual, and I identify as a freak."

"Do you worry about catching HIV?" a member of the audience asked him near the end of the show.

He was involved with the vampire subcultures in Chicago and Tampa, Florida. His 1998 appearance on *Jenny Jones* can be found online.

His work history was spotty. He worked primarily in grocery stores. He seemed drawn to the deli counter. The first few news articles that identified him speculated that he was a white nationalist, due to the vampire-skeleton face mask he wore during the attack and his pale complexion.

Despite being physically pale, he identified as black. The house he used for "training" displayed a number of flags including those of the Pan-African movement, Nazi Germany, Kekistan, and Gay Pride. He represented less a specific form of extremism, than all forms of extremism, or extremism itself.

John Merso uploaded sixteen videos to YouTube under the name Prophet88.

In the first video, titled *What It's Like to Be Albino*, he is sitting in a room under a poster of the band Tool and describes life as an albino man. "I was the outsider of the outsider, man, albino, goth, black, punk, gay, homeless, you name it."

His second video is a rant against Black Lives Matter. This video is called *Black Scams Matter*. He accuses the organization of being a "rip-off," and "in bed with Soros."

His third video, *What's Left of My House*, shows him walking through a moldy building, half-built, and complaining about a negative experience he had in attempting to build a house with his cousin, a project that "stalled out" after his cousin got arrested. He picks things up and puts them down, complaining about "water on everything."

John Merso's crimes never "grew legs," and is remembered mostly by the people of Moline, Illinois, and the families of those it affected; though, if you said, do you remember the albino guy who shot up the feminist bookstore in Moline, Illinois, news junkie types would probably remember and tell you exactly what they thought about the event.

The women who were killed were mocked online. The feminist bookstore where the shooting occurred appears to have been vaguely controversial in Moline, Illinois, and it can be assumed some locals were pleased to see the location repurposed.

Turning Pages was opened in 2013 by Wendy Deere-Lippman, a member of the Deere family, certainly the most famous family of Moline, Illinois.

Almost two hundred years earlier, her distant relative, John Deere, opened his namesake business and cultivated a family fortune that would support the opening of a feminist bookstore in Moline, Illinois (not exactly a hotbed of feminist activity), but that also contributed to controversy in a conservative community that associated John Deere, rightly or wrongly, with something passed, and the period before everything bewildering and new.

Several years before the shooting at Turning Pages, local controversy arose when it hosted a talk called "Shout Your Abortion." "Moline Shout Your Abortion, Brought To You By John Deere?" one Midwest newspaper reported. A few forum posts followed up. Some Facebook users chimed in. Nothing much seemed to come of it though.

After the shooting the owner of the business, Wendy Deere-Lippman appeared on local news. "We're going to get through this, and we will reopen," she said. It's unclear if that occurred. In any case, the website for the store now redirects to a search engine, and the Yelp page for Turning Pages indicates that the store has permanently closed.

In the fourth video John Merso uploaded, he is walking around Moline, Illinois. "It's March 22, man. I can't believe it man. I'm coming through again, yeah. Babies being born. They don't know nothing else. You are a broken pig, man. Black lives matters, I don't know, do they matters?"

John Merso was born to a black father and a white mother. His biography can be teased out of his many rants, recorded over a seven-year period. "My daddy never got off his ass. There's hate, there's an anger, man."

He was building a house on a plot of land he inherited, but at some point ran out of money. That unfinished house became "his work." His work was hanging out at the unfinished house and navigating around the many mannequins he shot at and sometimes even partially buried in the yard.

In one video he says, "have you ever seen this trick?" then holds a lighter up to a spraypaint can and blackens the face of a mannequin.

"My cousin was doing some work for me, but he stopped," he says, pointing to this failed house, half finished, in a field.

The house he was building was complexly strange, for one thing, no road appears to be connected to it. It almost looks fake, like a facade. When he opens the door, the outside light still comes in. The interior of the house is exposed to the elements. In videos he explores its maze of dirty rooms. The wind blew the flags around and a mannequin, toppled and incomplete, was covered in mildew.

He used this house for his "training" activities, as was reported in *The New York Times*. His channel was described as "howling missives from the heart of alienation." It was a banal and little-viewed mix of rants and action-like sequences in a first-person perspective. He ran through the unreal house screaming, sometimes at night, a light strapped to his head like an old-timey miner.

GRANDMOTHER

"My life is paradise now. I am the one I wished to be. I am all that I wanted to be."

Dill's grandmother got suddenly sick from drinking, and was in the hospital, dying.

She was a '60s hippie, a kind of person very old now, with prune-colored bruisings all over. In the face of death, she was waxing poetic, talking wildly.

Dill took her hand.

"I was born in 1938, I am a baby again, the kid I thought I was rapturous of, wow."

Spittle gathered at the ends of her mouth, like police at the edge of an auditorium, figuring how to shut down this unsettling talk. I tried to dim my bugeyes, worried I was in fact talking through this old dying woman, like a ventriloquist.

"I am walking through a house, yeah. Into dreams and delusions. Transcendence, yeah."

*

I began talking to myself at night, when I can't sleep and am going insane. "I have run from life. I have been terrified of life. I have lived in death. I was like that freakish man, he was me, in some future."

"Are you OK," Dill said.
"Let's go on a trip," I said to Dill.
"Where do you want to go,"
"Let's go to Salem, Massachusetts for Halloween."

*

Dill's grandmother died.

I bought a suit and went to the funeral. My dad attended also. Dill's Dad came out of the basement and met my dad. He seemed normal that day. They talked a little while.

There was a family feeling in things.

For a few months, in the heat and light of summer, my life became a dream, finer than I ever thought possible.

But I still stare into the window too much.

It's too much like a mirror.

DEAR MOM II

It's almost autumn again, and I guess I'm thinking about you. It took me a long time to think about the fact that you died. It was crazy that you died at the hands of a real lolcow like the guy that killed you. I wonder what you thought of Moline, Illinois in the hours and days prior to being killed. That was really the end of your life, huh? Based on what I pieced together, you were going to give a talk there, do a book signing. It sure looked like a crummy place. Your heart was a crummy place, Mom, and you have nothing to show for it. I couldn't sleep again last night, but at least the air coming in the window was nice. I don't have any air-conditioning.

I wonder what you'd think of my girlfriend. It's not serious and never will be. Though we may get married. Why not, I say. I don't take life particularly seriously.

Sometimes I'm not who I think I am. Does that make sense? I think the world may be ending soon. Are you familiar with this thing about the red heifers?

I'm engaging with a form of skepticism that is exciting to me, and maybe revolutionary for humanity. It rejects the legitimacy of almost all human activity, on the grounds that it is boring, absurd, ugly, and pointless, and pernicious to all that is nonhuman, and thus unjustifiable. I'm hoping things end, meaning everything. Are these crazy thoughts to have, or the default direction when a man's mind wanders away from the concrete?

Talk soon?
Armilus

MESSAGE FROM A STAR

On the day I died, I walked through jets of clear water. I have become like a hippie. I had a black look.

You have no idea how much energy it takes to deliver these tiny thoughts to you. It feels like throwing a football onto the moon.

Picture a jungle if all the leaves were blue.

John Merso is being punished here.

He is in love with you, my son, for reasons I cannot fathom.

Goodbye . . .

DILL

Dill and I got back together a few months ago, after that one bad night out. I wondered how many parties are occurring right now. I have lived through the most horrendous acts of animal and child abuse, just slept through it, as it occurred distantly. There is a sense I have of what art can be, and this conspiracy-like feeling of what it is not. There may come a day where I am a father and she is a mother, but that's too far away. It feels impossible to imagine. Where were you when JFK was killed? Where were you on September 11th? Can you agree with me that we need these things? That these are the events that bring us together, and that when they stop happening that's the time really to worry.

She said it's her dream to start a family one day. I didn't say it, but I thought this: sometimes dreams become a nightmare. Especially in America, where there are even more products than people, and we want to bring the world together, like mice in a bucket.

I think my fate and the fate of the world are all tied up together, and that this period and your death has been designed to move me through a sequence of events that I think will influence the future. I believe that everything in the world is tied together.

I decided that all of the difficulties I've had are only just training for this life or the next. I'll see you again and she'll see you too. You never met my girlfriend in life. She likes music. I always thought "rock" was pretty corny stuff, but she really likes old music like a band called Lycia and another band called Iron Curtain. They released a song in 1984 called "The Condos" that we like. There's a song I heard that makes me think of you. It's by Lou Reed and called "Families." He says, "Families often make each other cry. No, I don't think I'll come home much anymore." I guess it's not that interesting, but I felt something when I heard it, and decided I'd better let you know.

I don't know how you got to me, but at night I see you outside my window, like *Salem's Lot*, or whatever, but you're in the stars, and as clear as cold water, the ultimate "white feminist" now, fifty feet tall and carrying a knife in your hand.

I thought I went insane in eleventh grade because I had killed my son (long story), but the real reason I went insane is because I realized that the world is an illusion, and that if I believed I killed my son, I really and truly did, and for anything to become real, all I had to do was believe it. It has taken me years to come back to that idea, but I have it again, and can handle it—I can hold the idea in my hand—because I am stronger, and in your own way, you really did raise me.

Mom, hear me now. The world is an illusion, and at the same time it is not. To the degree it is not, it is contained inside me. The only world I will ever know is inside me, and I am called to become the master of the entire world.

I will see you again, inside of me, and we will be one. In the meantime, say a little prayer for the world, and for our family too. So many things are going to happen. I understand why you did what you did, and I hope you will be able to understand what I am going to do.

It will be for me, and for Dill, and for you.

Sometime soon, let's be a family again.

THE END

A game my boyfriend and I like playing is imagining we run the world. We go into the woods and it feels enchanted. His name is Armand. He's a little bit older, a little bit taller, in this dream. When I wake up tomorrow, I think we are going on a trip.

I fall back asleep, where I visit New York to talk with people connected with the release of my book. Or rather, I traveled to New York to discuss a new manuscript I wrote. But that was only in my dream, or not; maybe I would get that one day, or if not that, something else good, somehow better yet. The weirdest thing is somehow believing that anything is possible. He's back at home in this one, planning something odd, but it's so good it's bad, or the other way around . . .

I took my seat in the little auditorium.

The play was about the world, and was the world. The curtain rose and then fell, rustled like red velvet oceans. But there was something else still, some movement behind.

If we are content to be present, we will live here forever.